STRETCH ARMSTRONG AND THE FLEX FIGHTERS

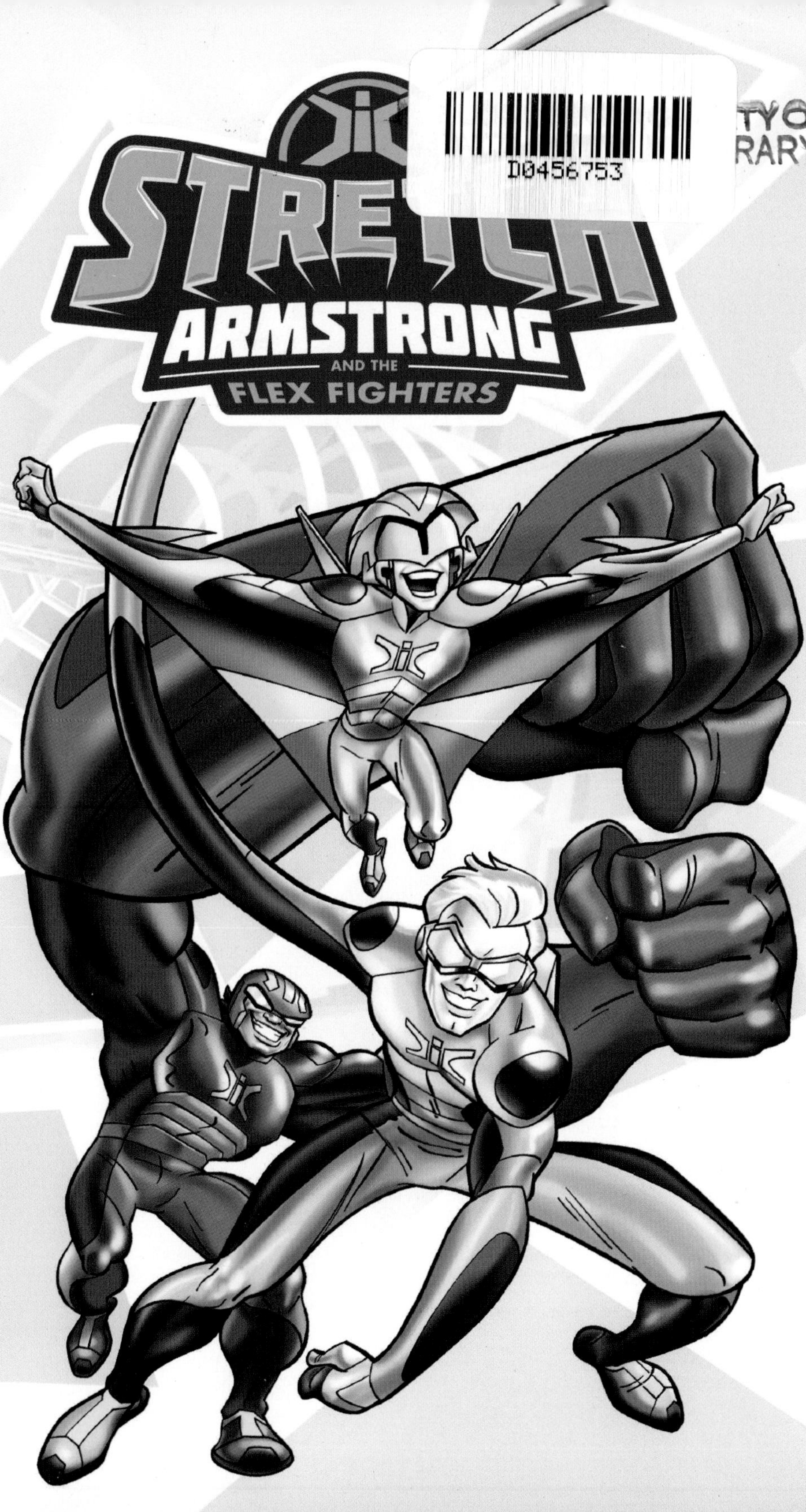

Become our fan on Facebook **facebook.com/idwpublishing**
Follow us on Twitter **@idwpublishing**
Subscribe to us on YouTube **youtube.com/idwpublishing**
See what's new on Tumblr **tumblr.idwpublishing.com**
Check us out on Instagram **instagram.com/idwpublishing**

IDW
www.IDWPUBLISHING.com

Licensed By:

Greg Goldstein, President & Publisher
Robbie Robbins, EVP & Sr. Art Director
Chris Ryall, Chief Creative Officer & Editor-in-Chief
Matthew Ruzicka, CPA, Chief Financial Officer
David Hedgecock, Associate Publisher
Laurie Windrow, Senior Vice President of Sales & Marketing
Lorelei Bunjes, VP of Digital Services
Eric Moss, Sr. Director, Licensing & Business Development

Ted Adams, Founder & CEO of IDW Media Holdings

COVER ARTIST
ALUIR AMANCIO

COLLECTION EDITORS
JUSTIN EISINGER
& ALONZO SIMON

COLLECTION DESIGNER
CLAUDIA CHONG

PUBLISHER
GREG GOLDSTEIN

ISBN: 978-1-68405-250-9   21 20 19 18   1 2 3 4

Originally published as STRETCH ARMSTRONG AND THE FLEX FIGHTERS
issues #1–3.

Special thanks to Elizabeth Artale, Derryl DePriest, Ed Lane, and Michael Kelly
for their invaluable assistance.

For international rights, contact licensing@idwpublishing.com

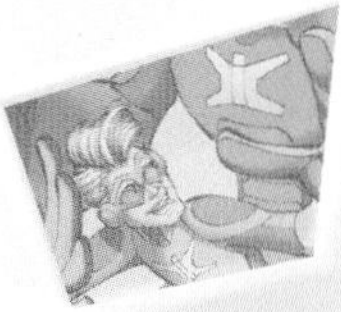
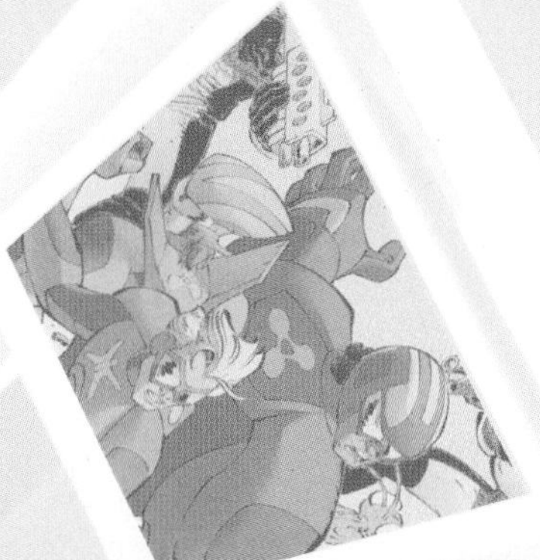

WRITERS
KEVIN BURKE & CHRIS "DOC" WYATT

ARTIST
NIKOS KOUTSIS

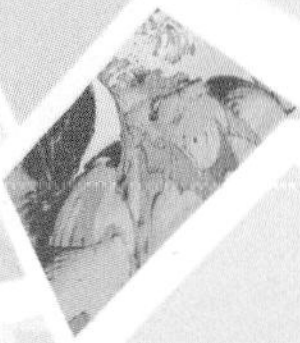

COLORIST
MIKE TORIS

LETTERER
CHRISTA MIESNER

SERIES EDITOR
JOE HUGHES

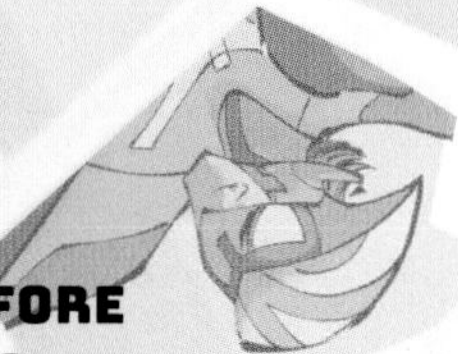

THIS STORY TAKES PLACE BEFORE
SEASON 1, EPISODE 8

OF THE NETFLIX SERIES

STRETCH ARMSTRONG
AND THE FLEX FIGHTERS

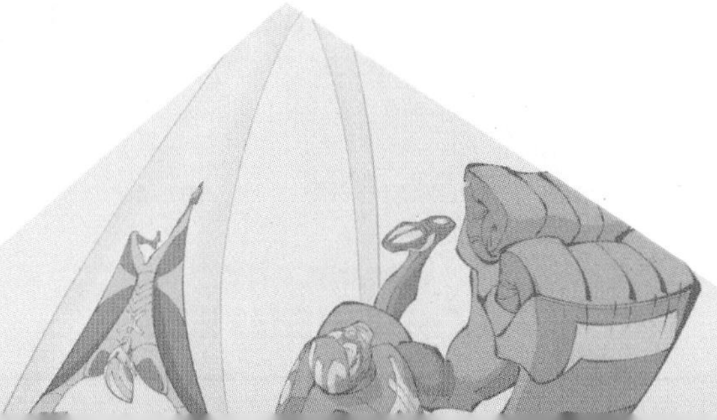

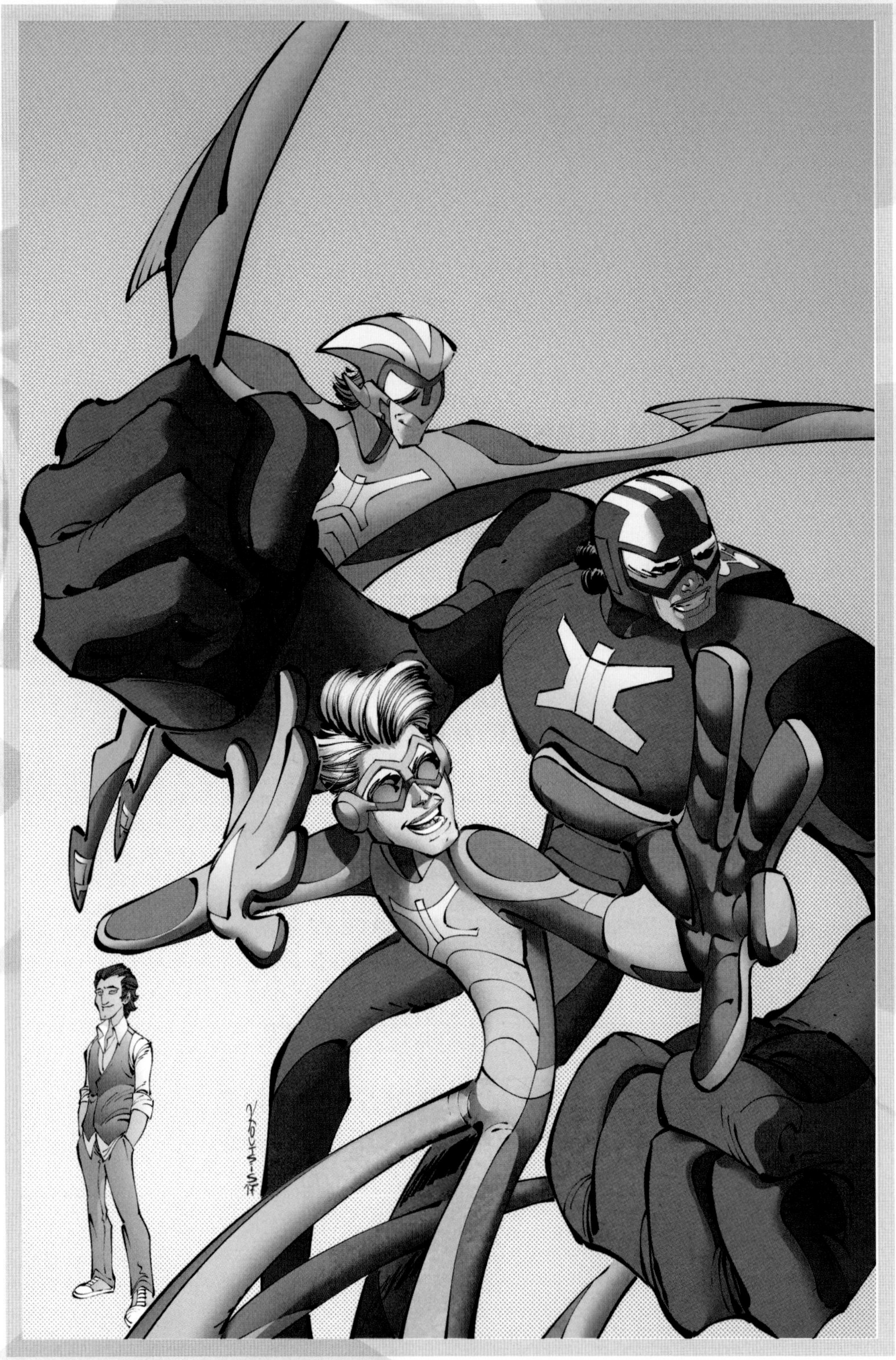

COVER ART
NIKOS KOUTSIS

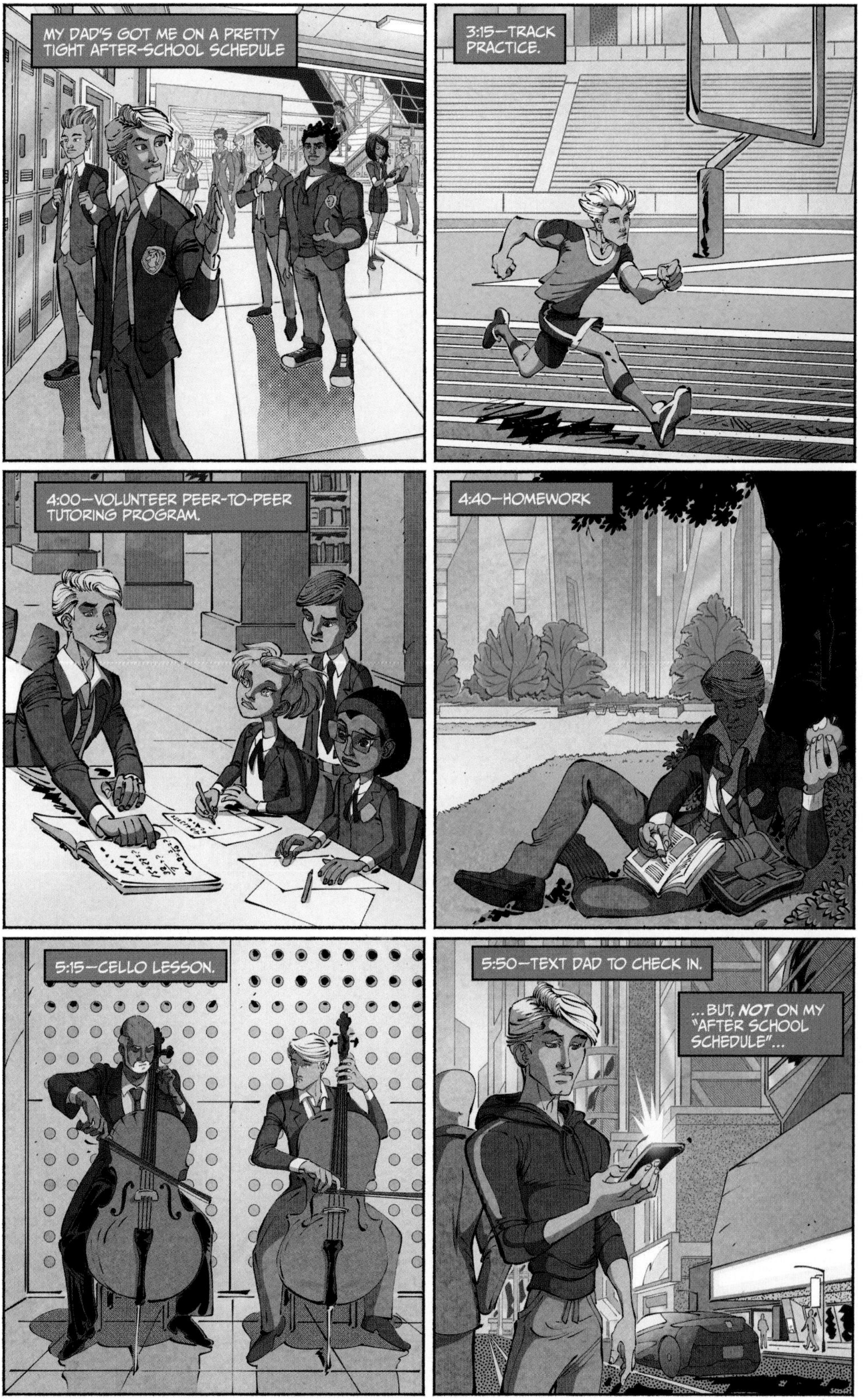
MY DAD'S GOT ME ON A PRETTY TIGHT AFTER-SCHOOL SCHEDULE
3:15—TRACK PRACTICE.
4:00—VOLUNTEER PEER-TO-PEER TUTORING PROGRAM.
4:40—HOMEWORK
5:15—CELLO LESSON.
5:50—TEXT DAD TO CHECK IN.
...BUT, *NOT* ON MY "AFTER SCHOOL SCHEDULE"...

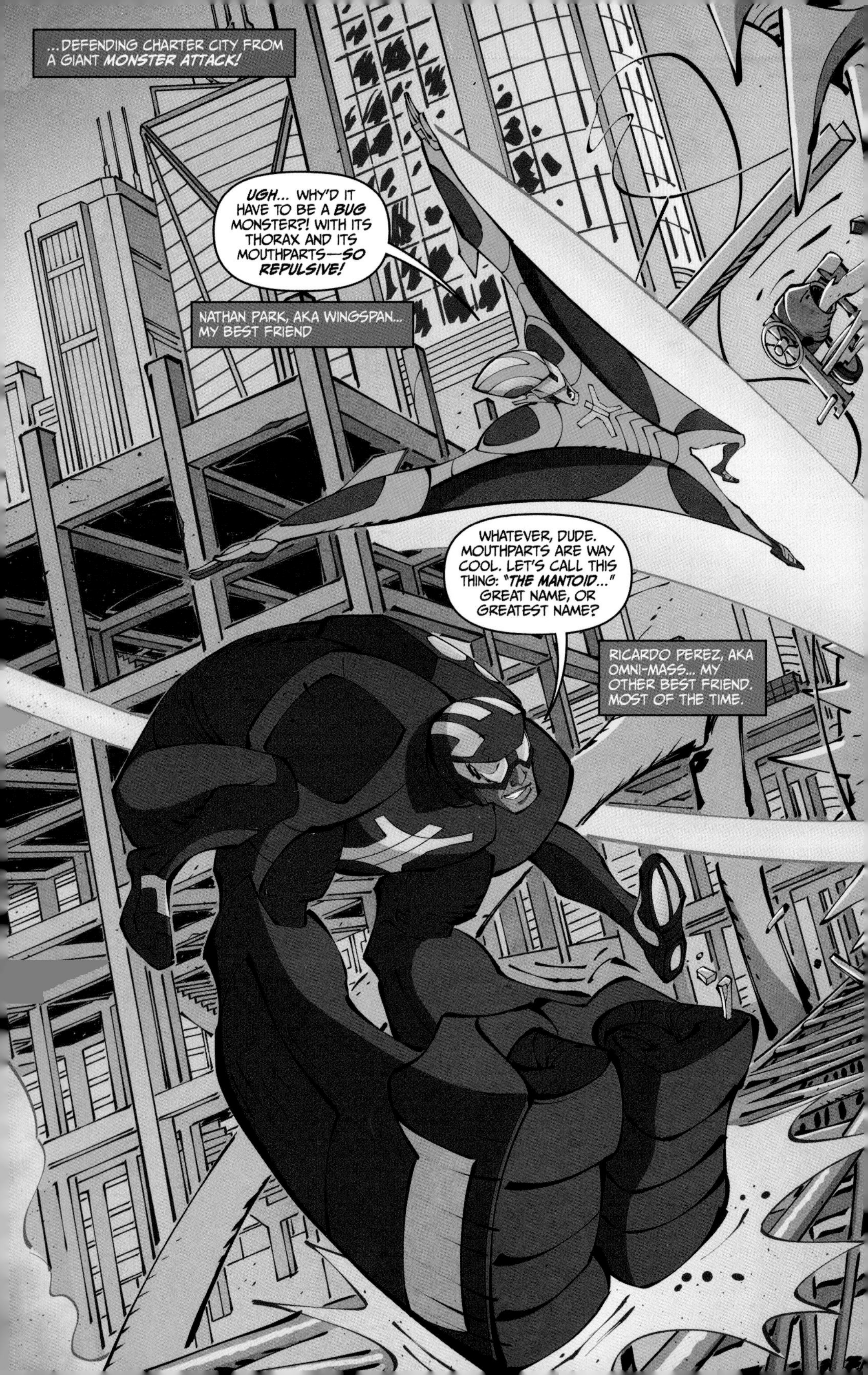
...DEFENDING CHARTER CITY FROM A GIANT MONSTER ATTACK!
UGH... WHY'D IT HAVE TO BE A BUG MONSTER?! WITH ITS THORAX AND ITS MOUTHPARTS—SO REPULSIVE!
NATHAN PARK, AKA WINGSPAN... MY BEST FRIEND
WHATEVER, DUDE. MOUTHPARTS ARE WAY COOL. LET'S CALL THIS THING: "THE MANTOID..." GREAT NAME, OR GREATEST NAME?
RICARDO PEREZ, AKA OMNI-MASS... MY OTHER BEST FRIEND. MOST OF THE TIME.

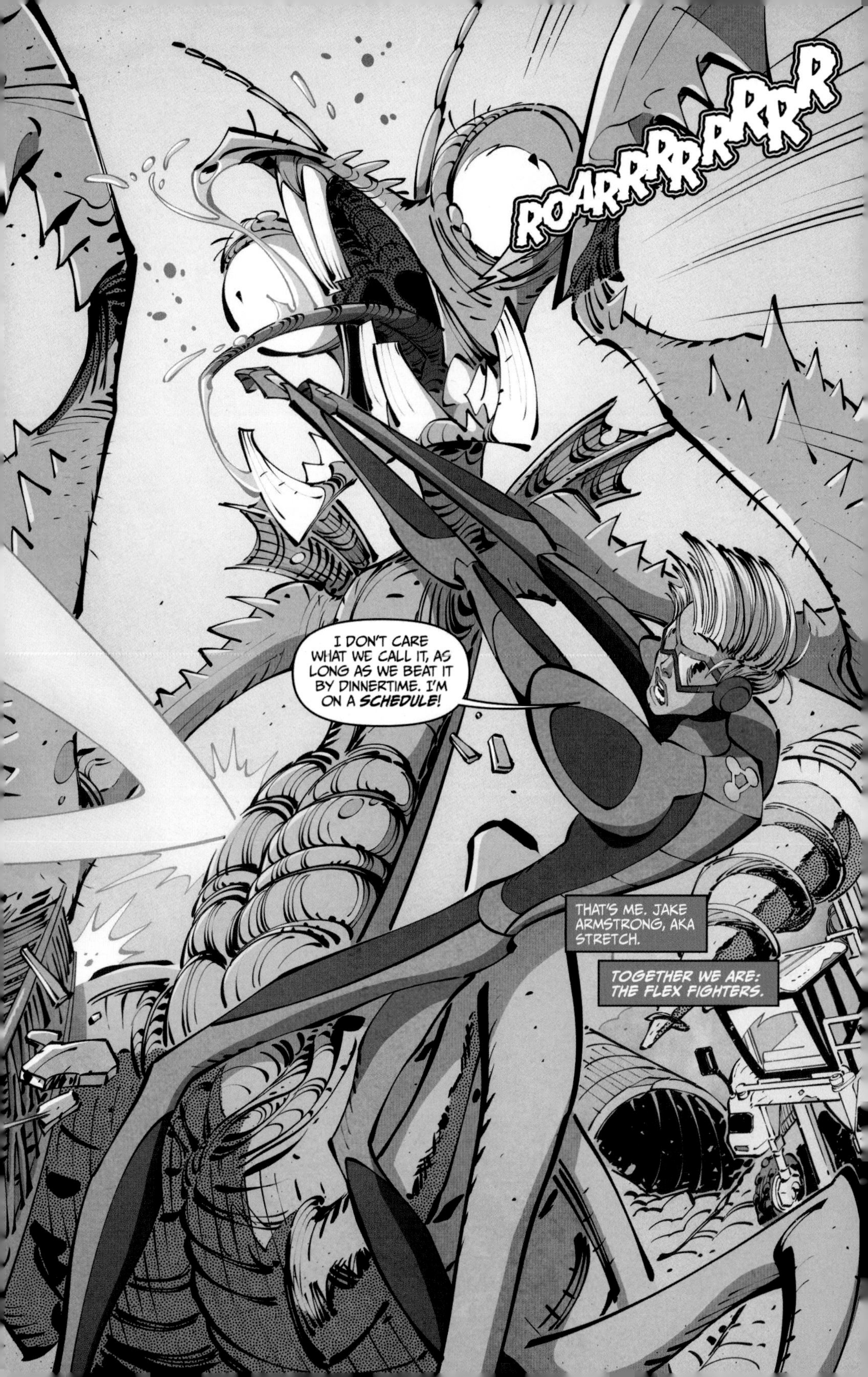
ROARRRRRRRRR
I DON'T CARE WHAT WE CALL IT, AS LONG AS WE BEAT IT BY DINNERTIME. I'M ON A SCHEDULE!
THAT'S ME. JAKE ARMSTRONG, AKA STRETCH.
TOGETHER WE ARE: THE FLEX FIGHTERS.

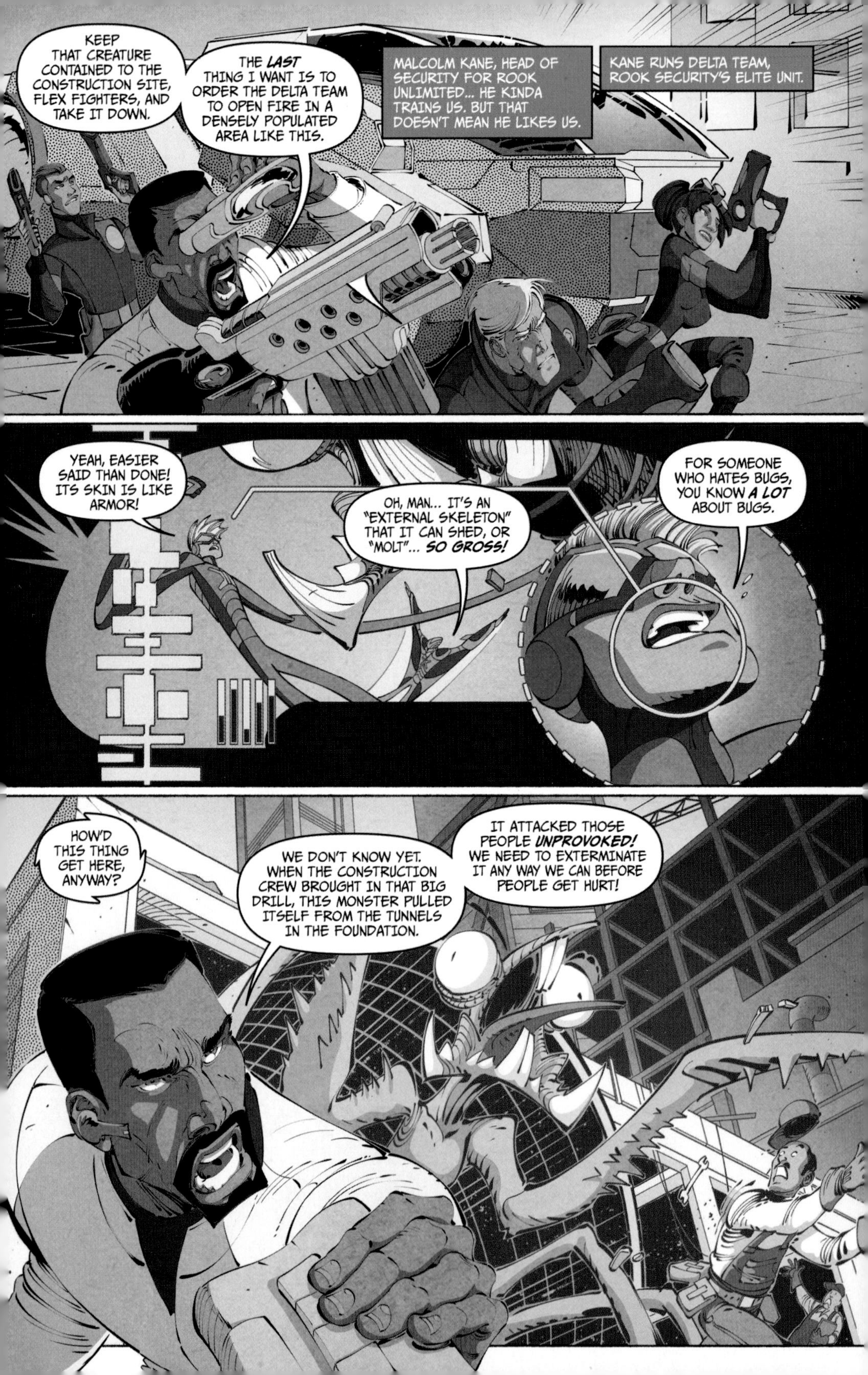
KEEP THAT CREATURE CONTAINED TO THE CONSTRUCTION SITE, FLEX FIGHTERS, AND TAKE IT DOWN.
THE *LAST* THING I WANT IS TO ORDER THE DELTA TEAM TO OPEN FIRE IN A DENSELY POPULATED AREA LIKE THIS.
MALCOLM KANE, HEAD OF SECURITY FOR ROOK UNLIMITED... HE KINDA TRAINS US. BUT THAT DOESN'T MEAN HE LIKES US.
KANE RUNS DELTA TEAM, ROOK SECURITY'S ELITE UNIT.
YEAH, EASIER SAID THAN DONE! ITS SKIN IS LIKE ARMOR!
OH, MAN... IT'S AN "EXTERNAL SKELETON" THAT IT CAN SHED, OR "MOLT"... ***SO GROSS!***
FOR SOMEONE WHO HATES BUGS, YOU KNOW ***A LOT*** ABOUT BUGS.
HOW'D THIS THING GET HERE, ANYWAY?
WE DON'T KNOW YET. WHEN THE CONSTRUCTION CREW BROUGHT IN THAT BIG DRILL, THIS MONSTER PULLED ITSELF FROM THE TUNNELS IN THE FOUNDATION.
IT ATTACKED THOSE PEOPLE ***UNPROVOKED!*** WE NEED TO EXTERMINATE IT ANY WAY WE CAN BEFORE PEOPLE GET HURT!

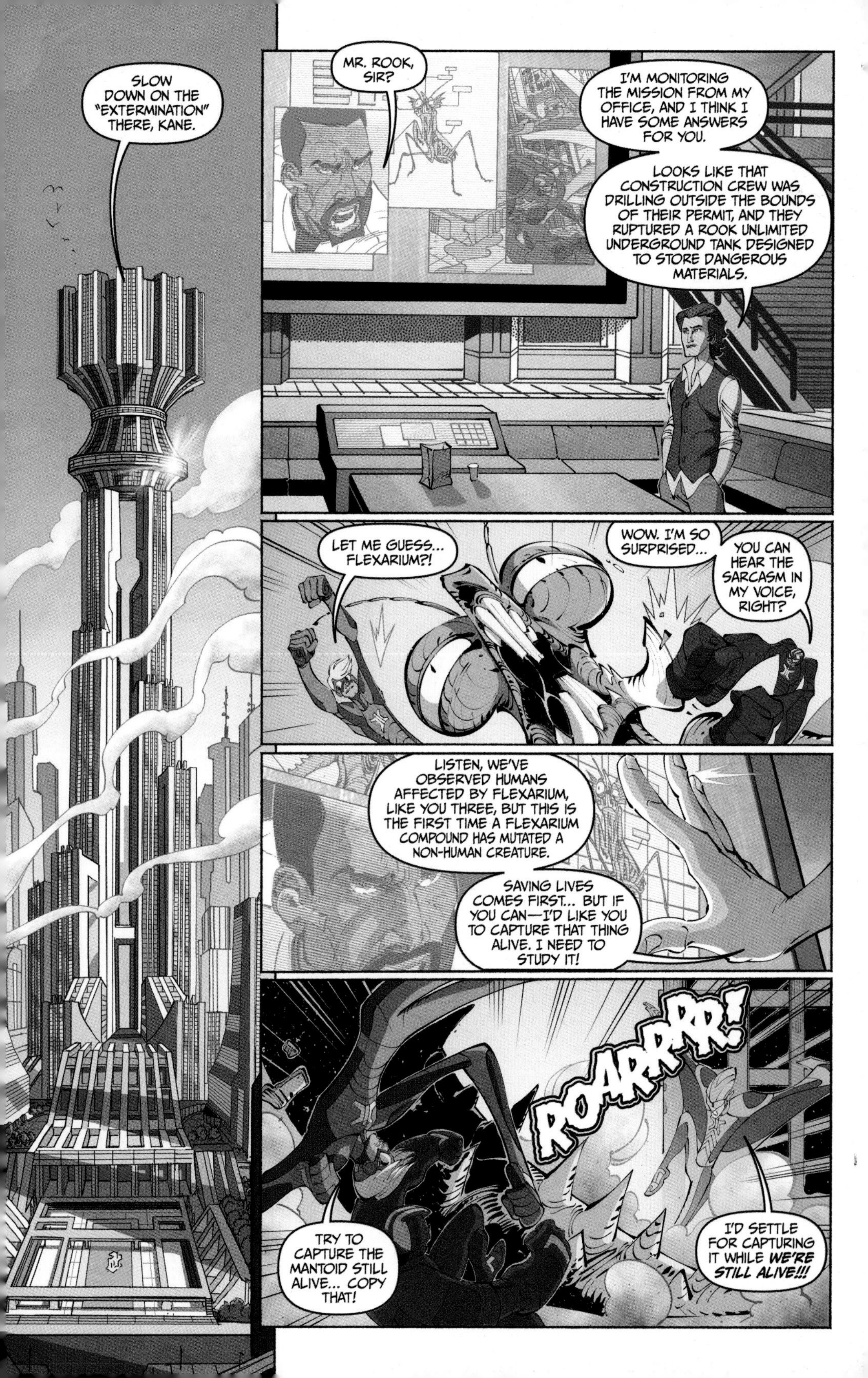
SLOW DOWN ON THE "EXTERMINATION" THERE, KANE.
MR. ROOK, SIR?
I'M MONITORING THE MISSION FROM MY OFFICE, AND I THINK I HAVE SOME ANSWERS FOR YOU.
LOOKS LIKE THAT CONSTRUCTION CREW WAS DRILLING OUTSIDE THE BOUNDS OF THEIR PERMIT, AND THEY RUPTURED A ROOK UNLIMITED UNDERGROUND TANK DESIGNED TO STORE DANGEROUS MATERIALS.
LET ME GUESS... FLEXARIUM?!
WOW. I'M SO SURPRISED...
YOU CAN HEAR THE SARCASM IN MY VOICE, RIGHT?
LISTEN, WE'VE OBSERVED HUMANS AFFECTED BY FLEXARIUM, LIKE YOU THREE, BUT THIS IS THE FIRST TIME A FLEXARIUM COMPOUND HAS MUTATED A NON-HUMAN CREATURE.
SAVING LIVES COMES FIRST... BUT IF YOU CAN—I'D LIKE YOU TO CAPTURE THAT THING ALIVE. I NEED TO STUDY IT!
ROARRRR!
TRY TO CAPTURE THE MANTOID STILL ALIVE... COPY THAT!
I'D SETTLE FOR CAPTURING IT WHILE *WE'RE STILL ALIVE!!!*

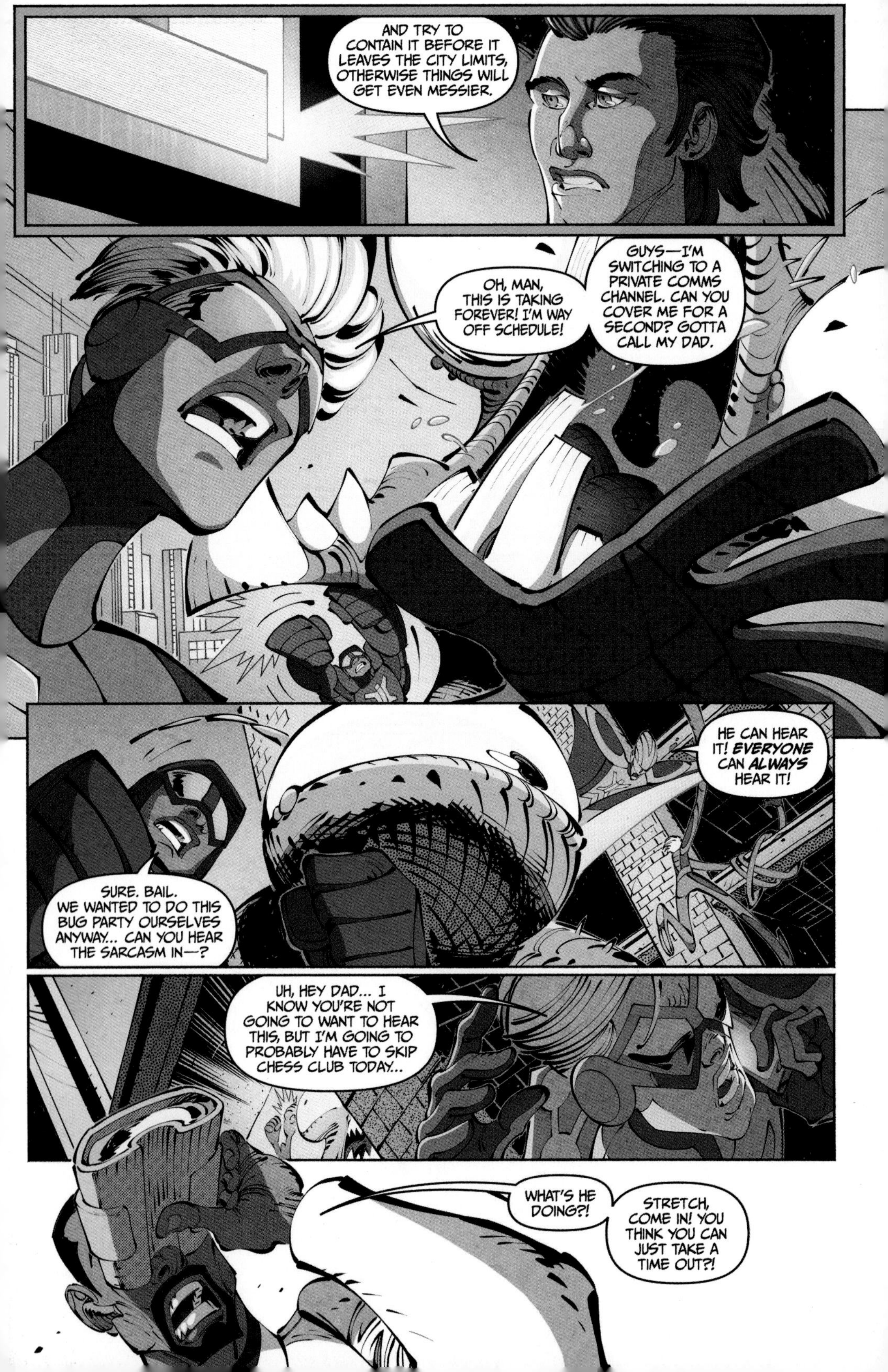
AND TRY TO CONTAIN IT BEFORE IT LEAVES THE CITY LIMITS, OTHERWISE THINGS WILL GET EVEN MESSIER.
OH, MAN, THIS IS TAKING FOREVER! I'M WAY OFF SCHEDULE!
GUYS—I'M SWITCHING TO A PRIVATE COMMS CHANNEL. CAN YOU COVER ME FOR A SECOND? GOTTA CALL MY DAD.
SURE. BAIL. WE WANTED TO DO THIS BUG PARTY OURSELVES ANYWAY... CAN YOU HEAR THE SARCASM IN—?
HE CAN HEAR IT! *EVERYONE* CAN *ALWAYS* HEAR IT!
UH, HEY DAD... I KNOW YOU'RE NOT GOING TO WANT TO HEAR THIS, BUT I'M GOING TO PROBABLY HAVE TO SKIP CHESS CLUB TODAY...
WHAT'S HE DOING?!
STRETCH, COME IN! YOU THINK YOU CAN JUST TAKE A TIME OUT?!

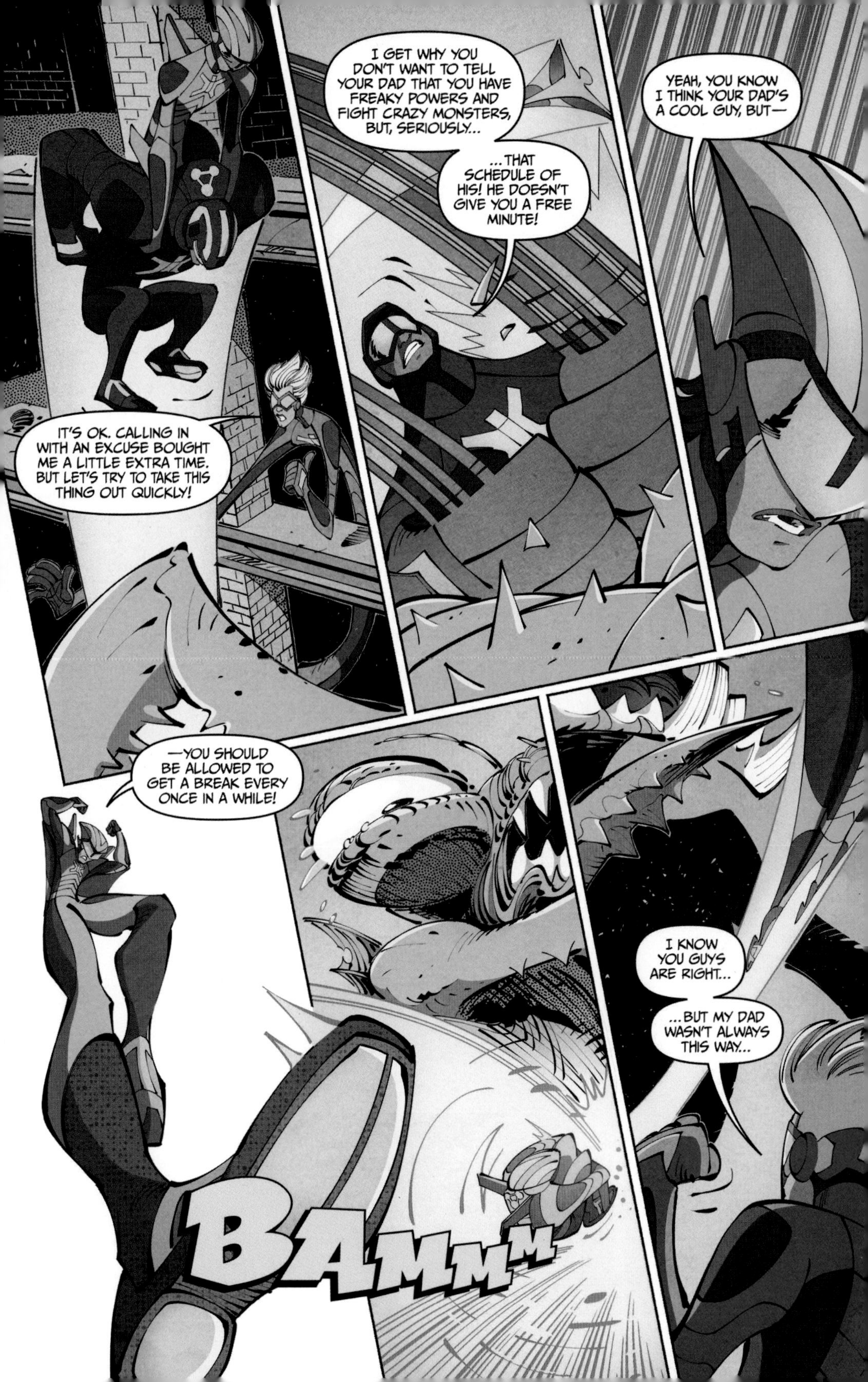
I GET WHY YOU DON'T WANT TO TELL YOUR DAD THAT YOU HAVE FREAKY POWERS AND FIGHT CRAZY MONSTERS, BUT, SERIOUSLY...
...THAT SCHEDULE OF HIS! HE DOESN'T GIVE YOU A FREE MINUTE!
YEAH, YOU KNOW I THINK YOUR DAD'S A COOL GUY, BUT—
IT'S OK. CALLING IN WITH AN EXCUSE BOUGHT ME A LITTLE EXTRA TIME. BUT LET'S TRY TO TAKE THIS THING OUT QUICKLY!
—YOU SHOULD BE ALLOWED TO GET A BREAK EVERY ONCE IN A WHILE!
BAMMMM
I KNOW YOU GUYS ARE RIGHT...
...BUT MY DAD WASN'T ALWAYS THIS WAY...

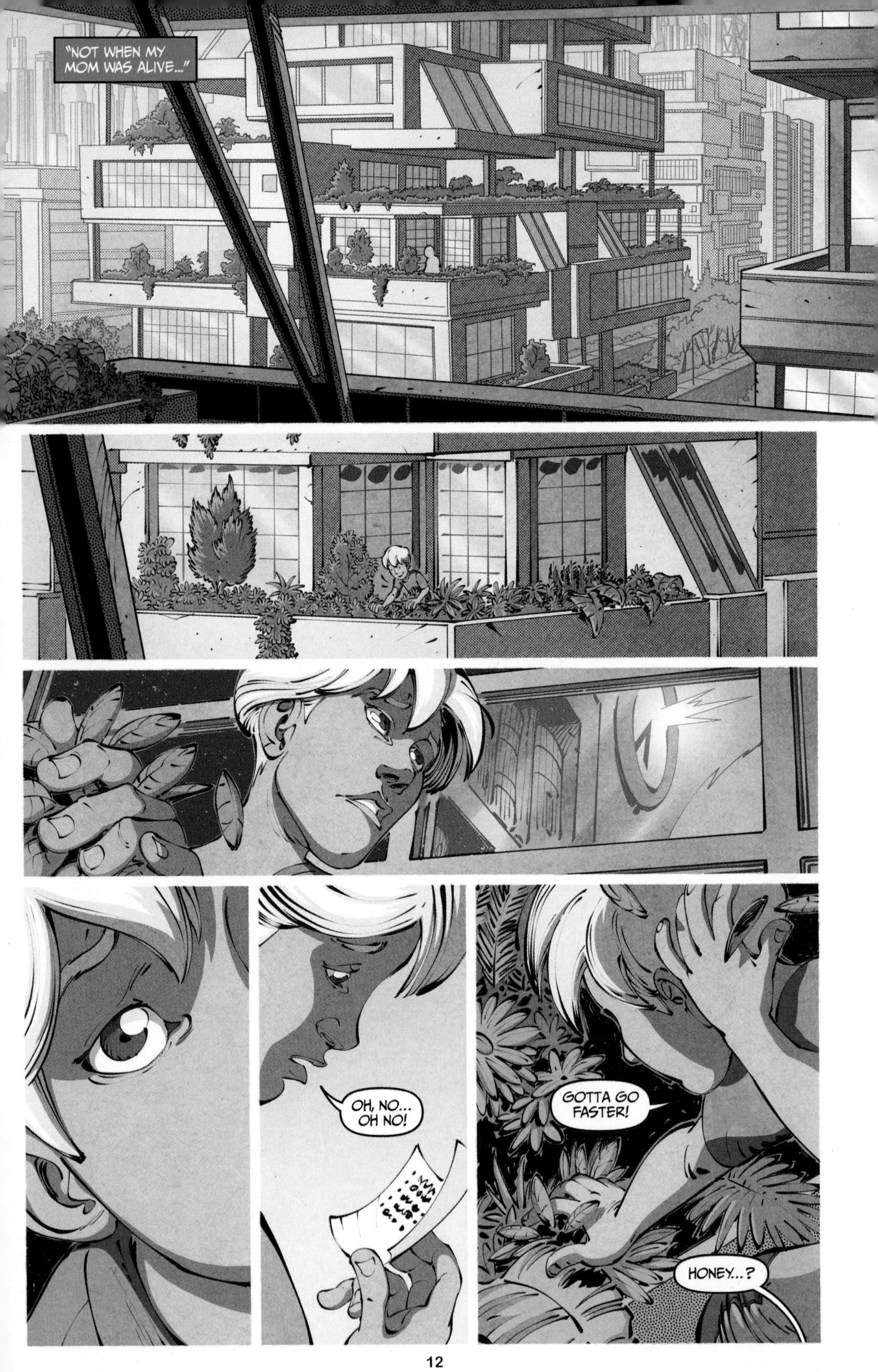
"NOT WHEN MY MOM WAS ALIVE..."
OH, NO... OH NO!
GOTTA GO FASTER!
HONEY...?

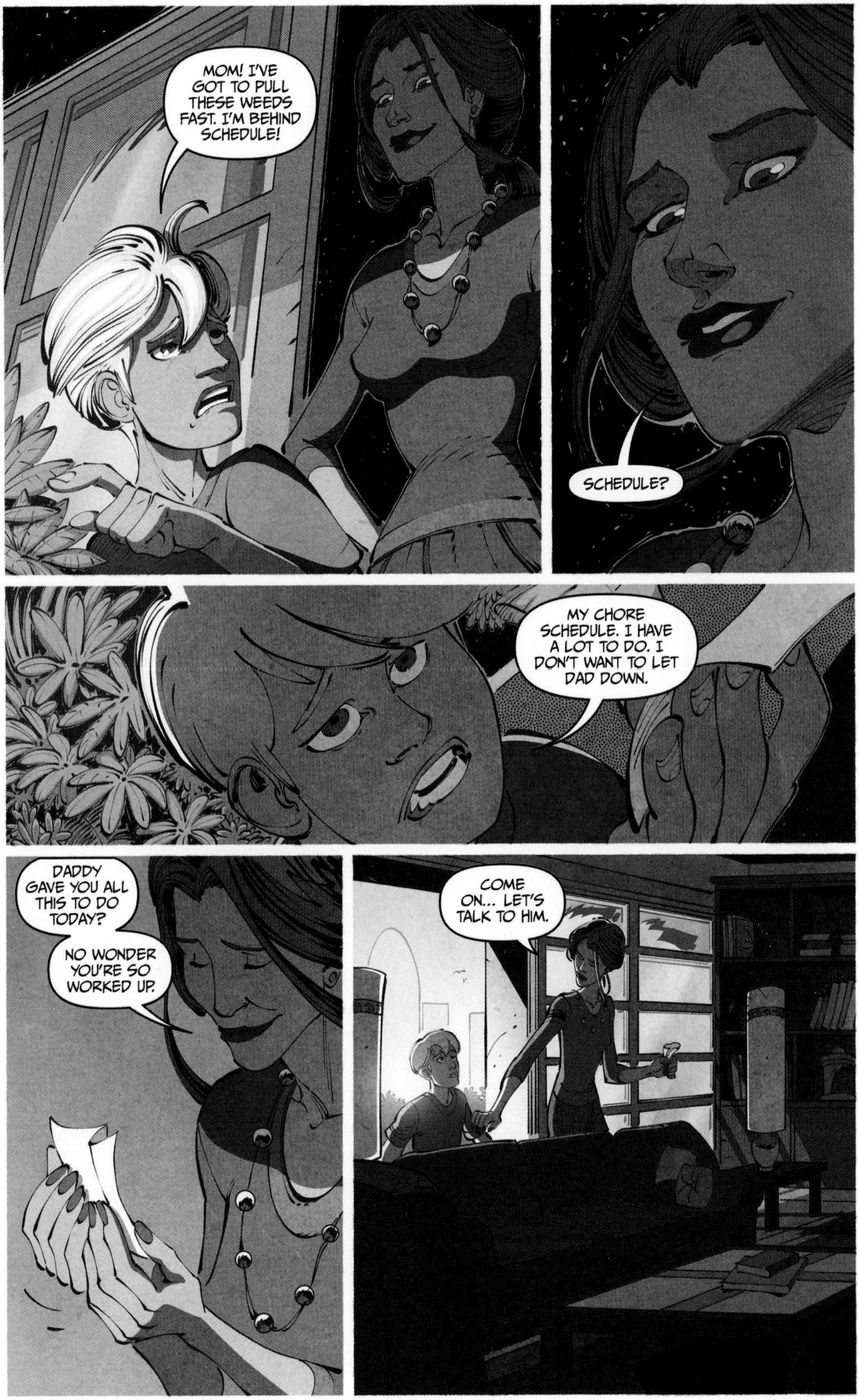
MOM! I'VE GOT TO PULL THESE WEEDS FAST. I'M BEHIND SCHEDULE!
SCHEDULE?
MY CHORE SCHEDULE. I HAVE A LOT TO DO. I DON'T WANT TO LET DAD DOWN.
DADDY GAVE YOU ALL THIS TO DO TODAY?
NO WONDER YOU'RE SO WORKED UP.
COME ON... LET'S TALK TO HIM.

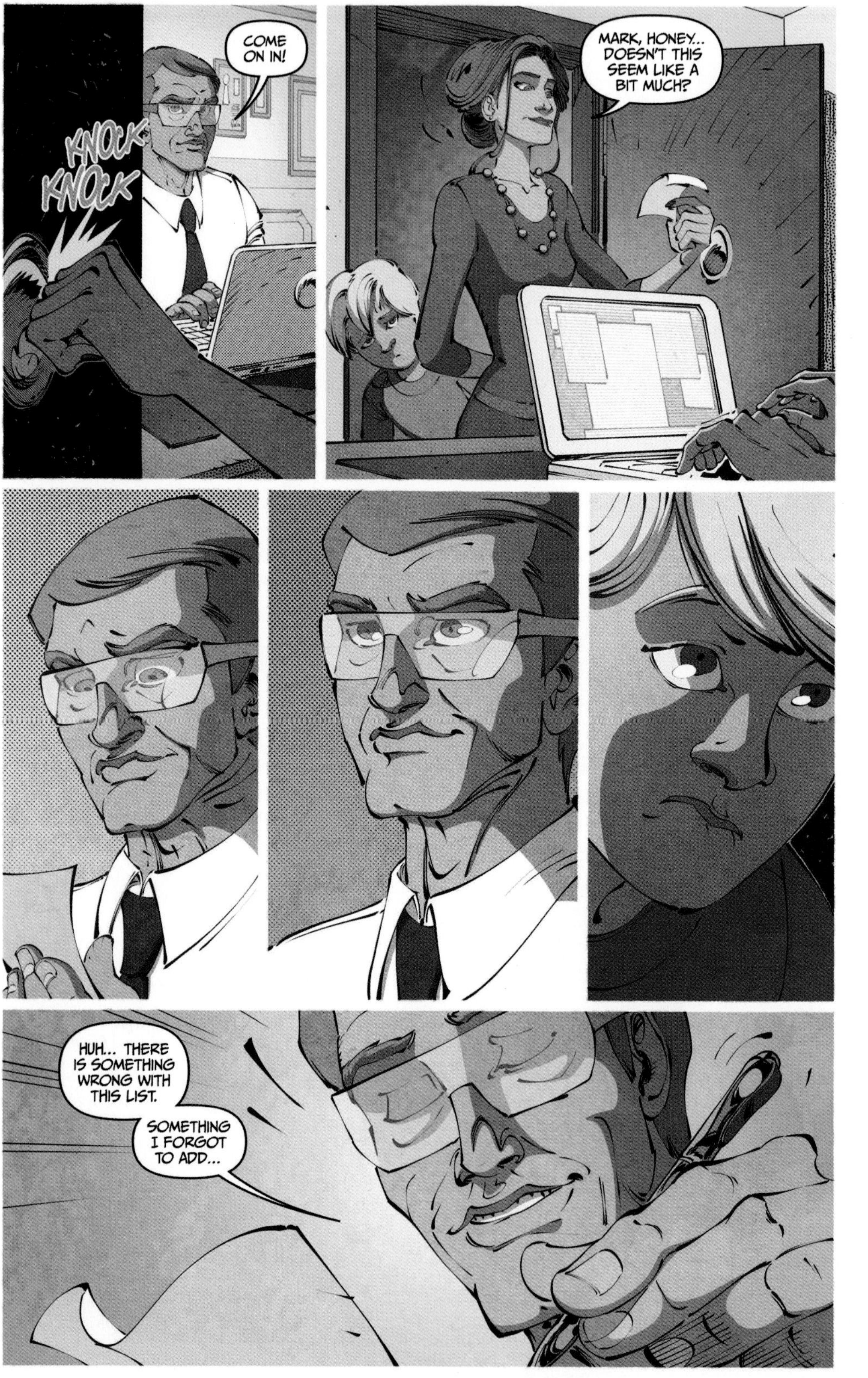
COME ON IN!
KNOCK KNOCK
MARK, HONEY... DOESN'T THIS SEEM LIKE A BIT MUCH?
HUH... THERE IS SOMETHING WRONG WITH THIS LIST.
SOMETHING I FORGOT TO ADD...

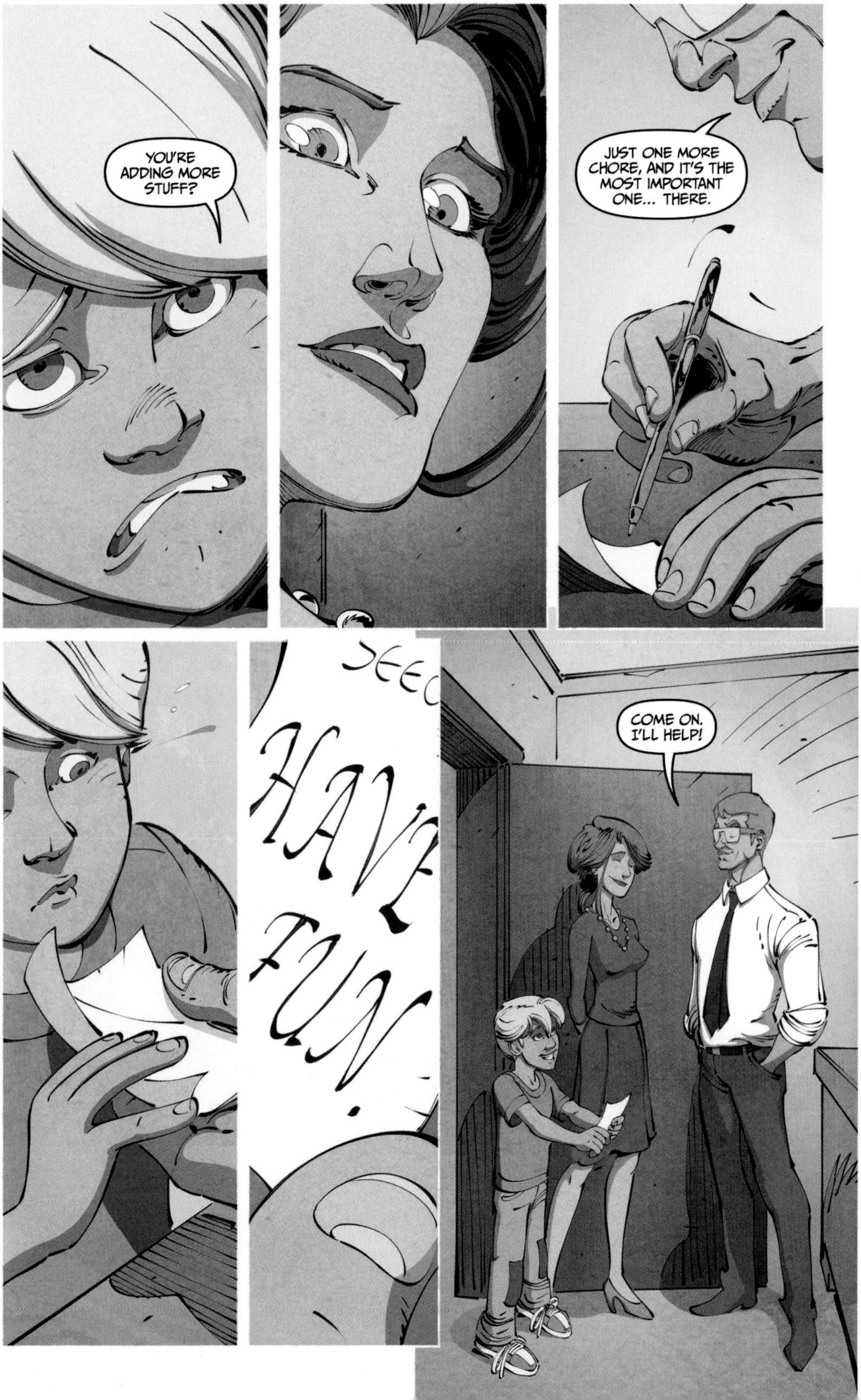
YOU'RE ADDING MORE STUFF?
JUST ONE MORE CHORE, AND IT'S THE MOST IMPORTANT ONE... THERE.
HAVE FUN.
COME ON. I'LL HELP!

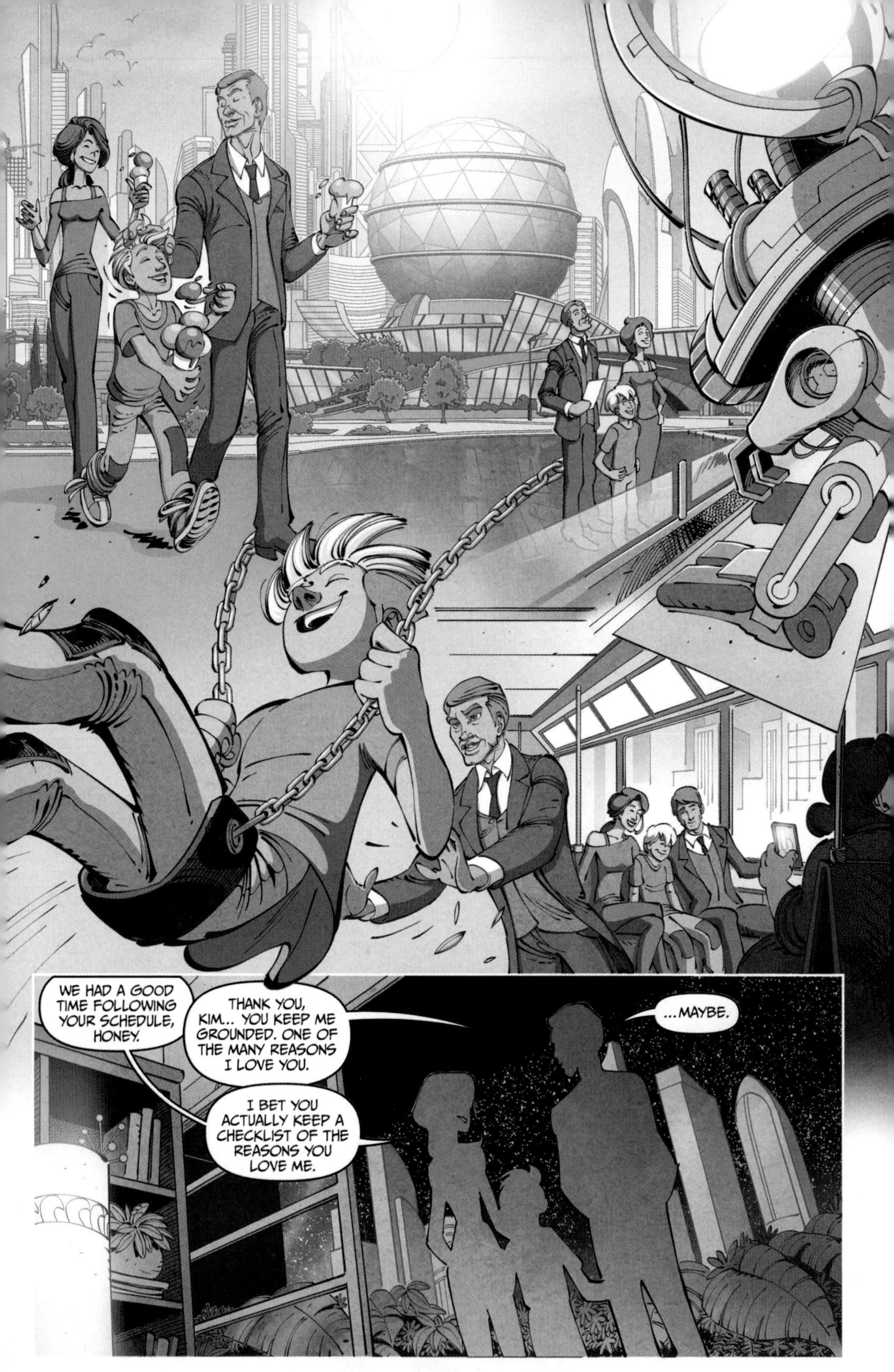
WE HAD A GOOD TIME FOLLOWING YOUR SCHEDULE, HONEY.
THANK YOU, KIM... YOU KEEP ME GROUNDED. ONE OF THE MANY REASONS I LOVE YOU.
I BET YOU ACTUALLY KEEP A CHECKLIST OF THE REASONS YOU LOVE ME.
...MAYBE.

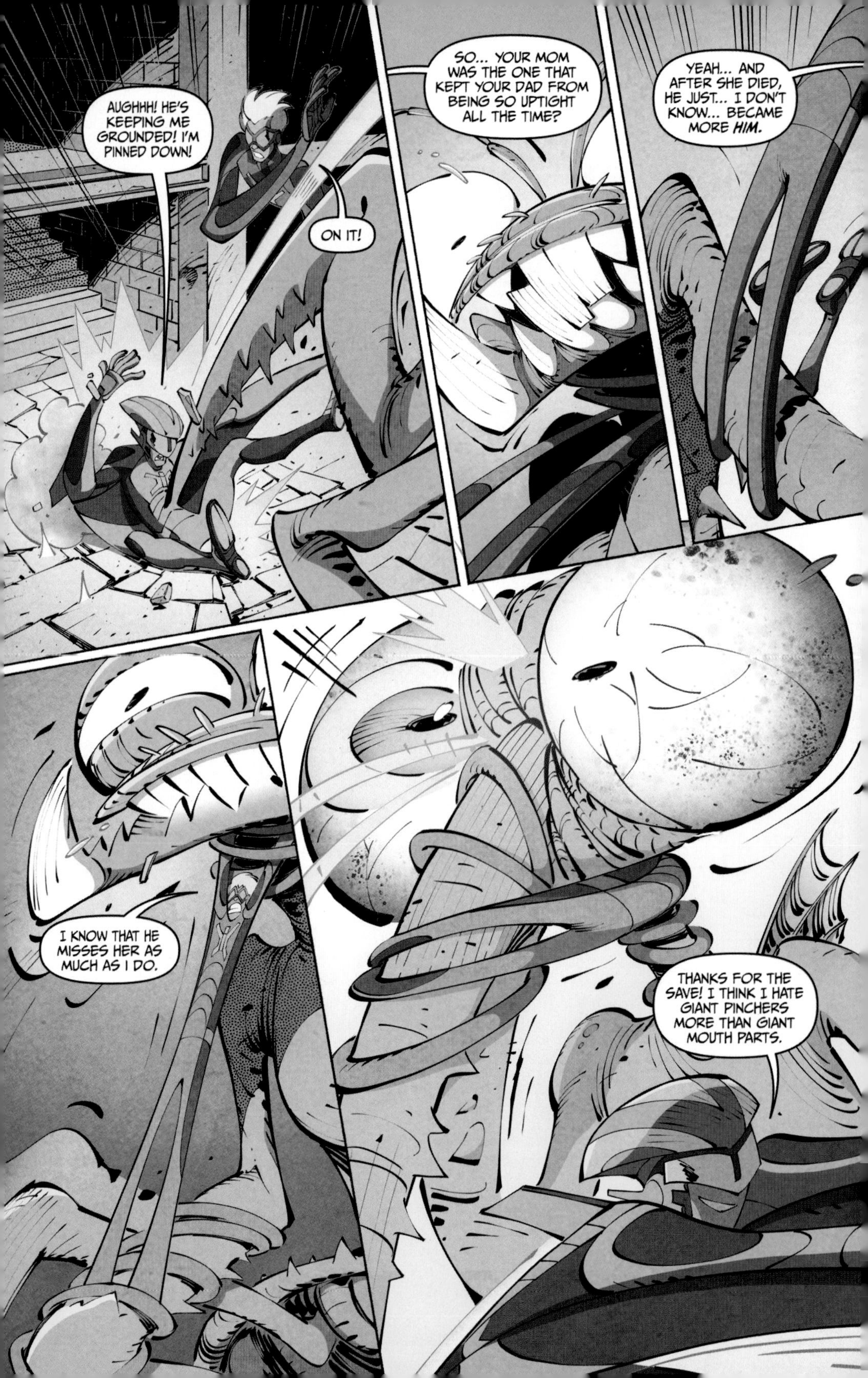
AUGHHH! HE'S KEEPING ME GROUNDED! I'M PINNED DOWN!
ON IT!
SO... YOUR MOM WAS THE ONE THAT KEPT YOUR DAD FROM BEING SO UPTIGHT ALL THE TIME?
YEAH... AND AFTER SHE DIED, HE JUST... I DON'T KNOW... BECAME MORE *HIM.*
I KNOW THAT HE MISSES HER AS MUCH AS I DO.
THANKS FOR THE SAVE! I THINK I HATE GIANT PINCHERS MORE THAN GIANT MOUTH PARTS.

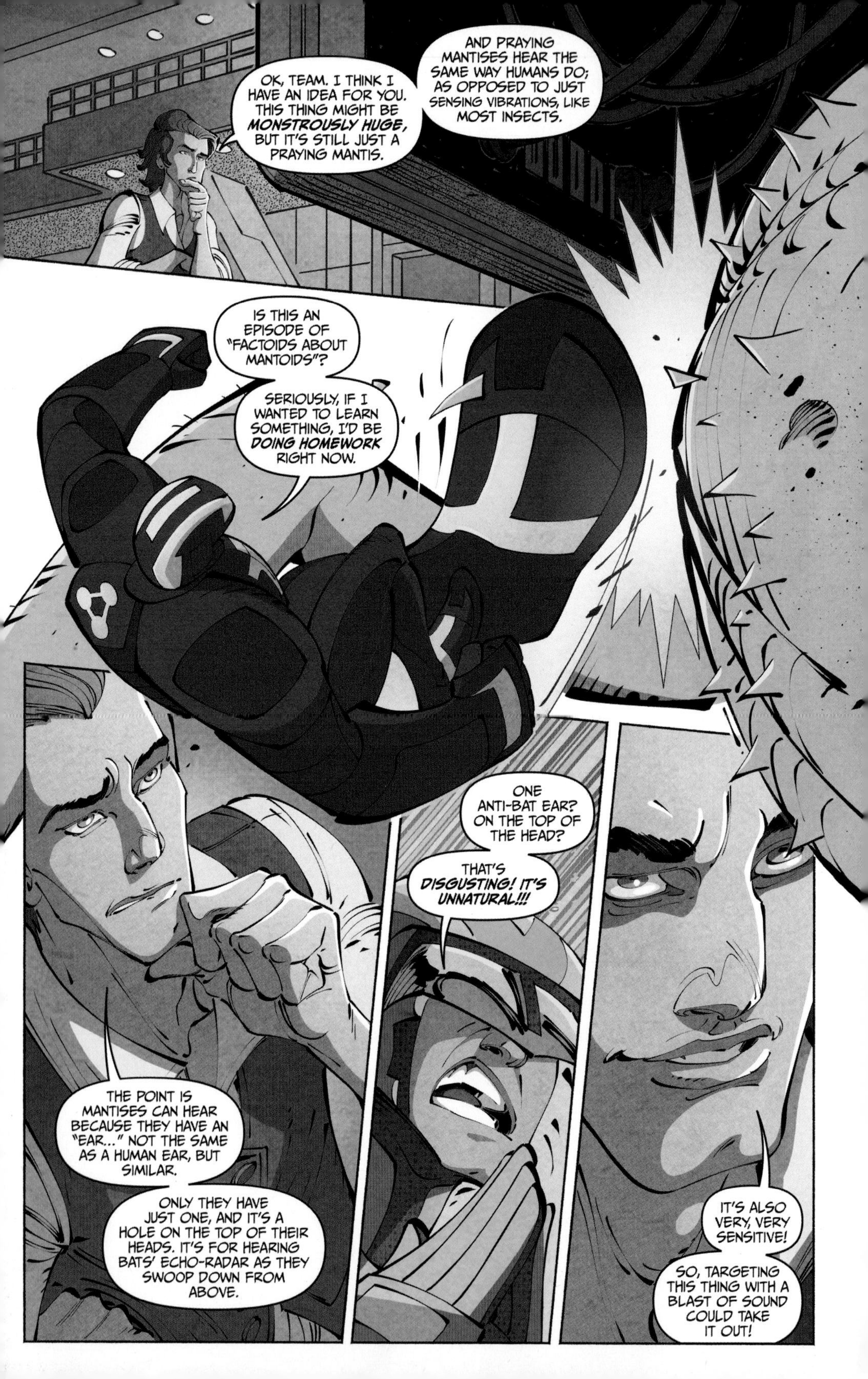
OK, TEAM. I THINK I HAVE AN IDEA FOR YOU. THIS THING MIGHT BE MONSTROUSLY HUGE, BUT IT'S STILL JUST A PRAYING MANTIS.
AND PRAYING MANTISES HEAR THE SAME WAY HUMANS DO; AS OPPOSED TO JUST SENSING VIBRATIONS, LIKE MOST INSECTS.
IS THIS AN EPISODE OF "FACTOIDS ABOUT MANTOIDS"?
SERIOUSLY, IF I WANTED TO LEARN SOMETHING, I'D BE DOING HOMEWORK RIGHT NOW.
THE POINT IS MANTISES CAN HEAR BECAUSE THEY HAVE AN "EAR..." NOT THE SAME AS A HUMAN EAR, BUT SIMILAR.
ONLY THEY HAVE JUST ONE, AND IT'S A HOLE ON THE TOP OF THEIR HEADS. IT'S FOR HEARING BATS' ECHO-RADAR AS THEY SWOOP DOWN FROM ABOVE.
ONE ANTI-BAT EAR? ON THE TOP OF THE HEAD?
THAT'S DISGUSTING! IT'S UNNATURAL!!!
IT'S ALSO VERY, VERY SENSITIVE!
SO, TARGETING THIS THING WITH A BLAST OF SOUND COULD TAKE IT OUT!

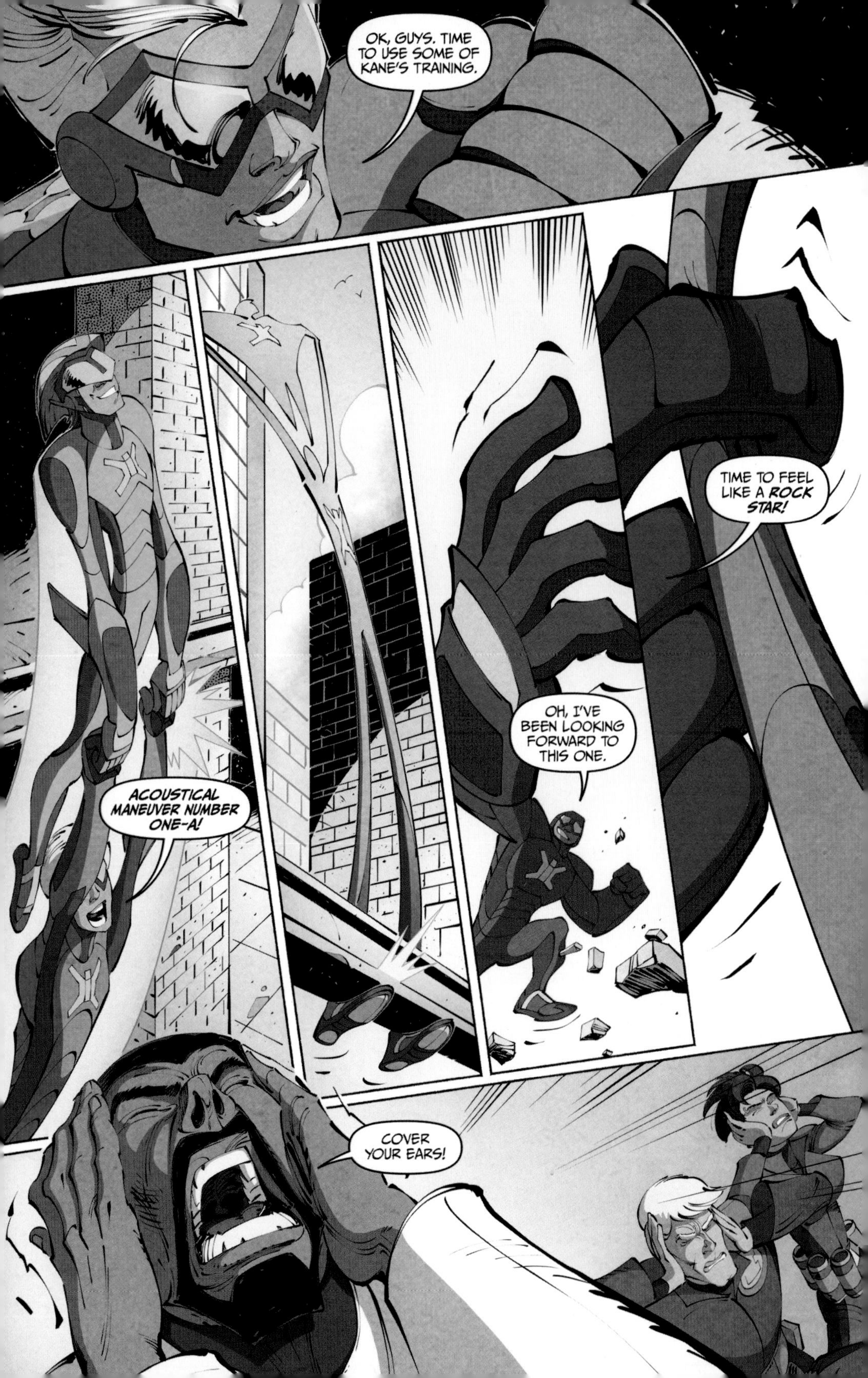
OK, GUYS. TIME TO USE SOME OF KANE'S TRAINING.
TIME TO FEEL LIKE A ROCK STAR!
OH, I'VE BEEN LOOKING FORWARD TO THIS ONE.
ACOUSTICAL MANEUVER NUMBER ONE-A!
COVER YOUR EARS!

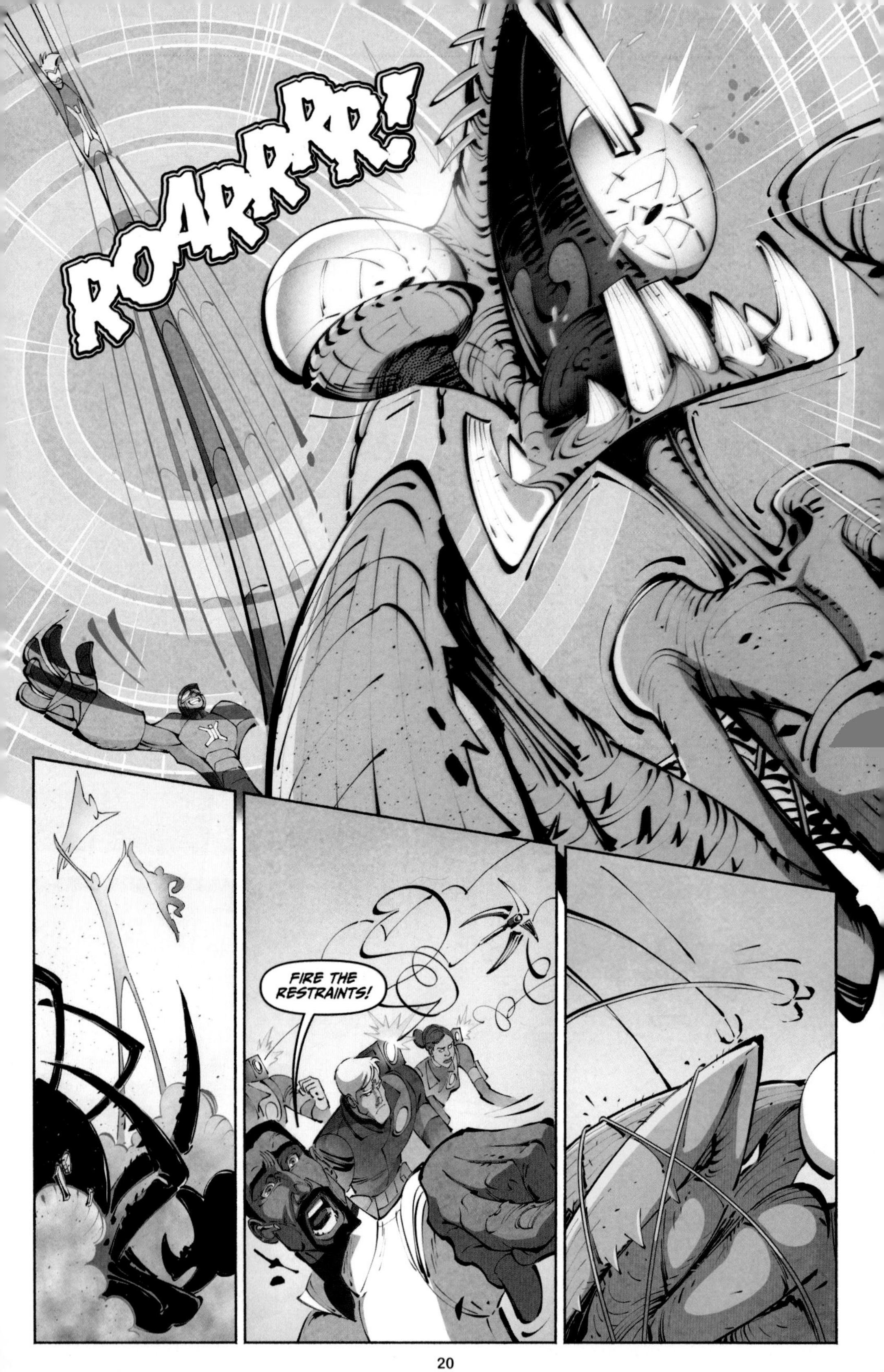
ROARRRR!
FIRE THE RESTRAINTS!

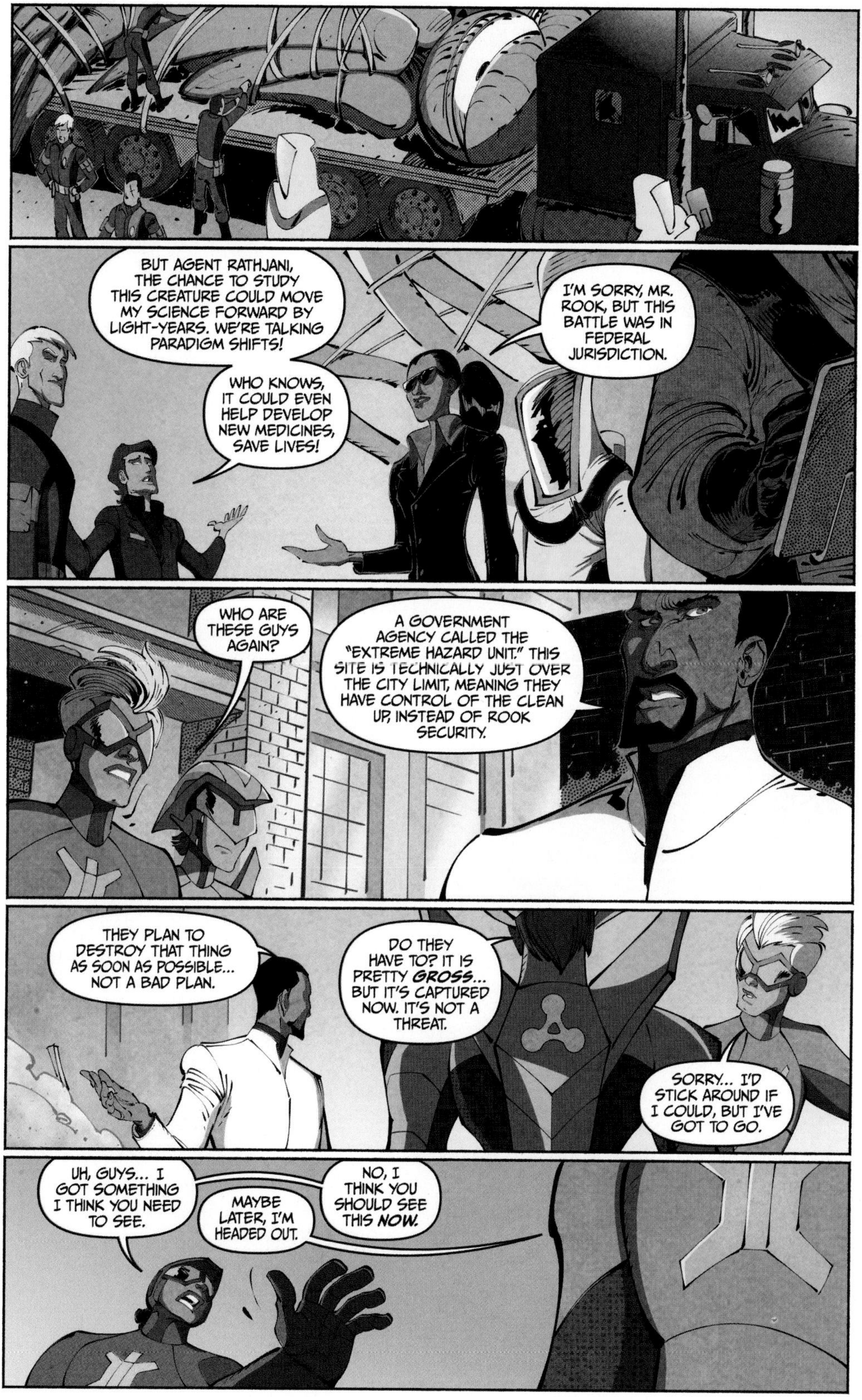
BUT AGENT RATHJANI, THE CHANCE TO STUDY THIS CREATURE COULD MOVE MY SCIENCE FORWARD BY LIGHT-YEARS. WE'RE TALKING PARADIGM SHIFTS!
WHO KNOWS, IT COULD EVEN HELP DEVELOP NEW MEDICINES, SAVE LIVES!
I'M SORRY, MR. ROOK, BUT THIS BATTLE WAS IN FEDERAL JURISDICTION.
WHO ARE THESE GUYS AGAIN?
A GOVERNMENT AGENCY CALLED THE "EXTREME HAZARD UNIT." THIS SITE IS TECHNICALLY JUST OVER THE CITY LIMIT, MEANING THEY HAVE CONTROL OF THE CLEAN UP, INSTEAD OF ROOK SECURITY.
THEY PLAN TO DESTROY THAT THING AS SOON AS POSSIBLE... NOT A BAD PLAN.
DO THEY HAVE TO? IT IS PRETTY GROSS... BUT IT'S CAPTURED NOW. IT'S NOT A THREAT.
SORRY... I'D STICK AROUND IF I COULD, BUT I'VE GOT TO GO.
UH, GUYS... I GOT SOMETHING I THINK YOU NEED TO SEE.
MAYBE LATER, I'M HEADED OUT.
NO, I THINK YOU SHOULD SEE THIS NOW.

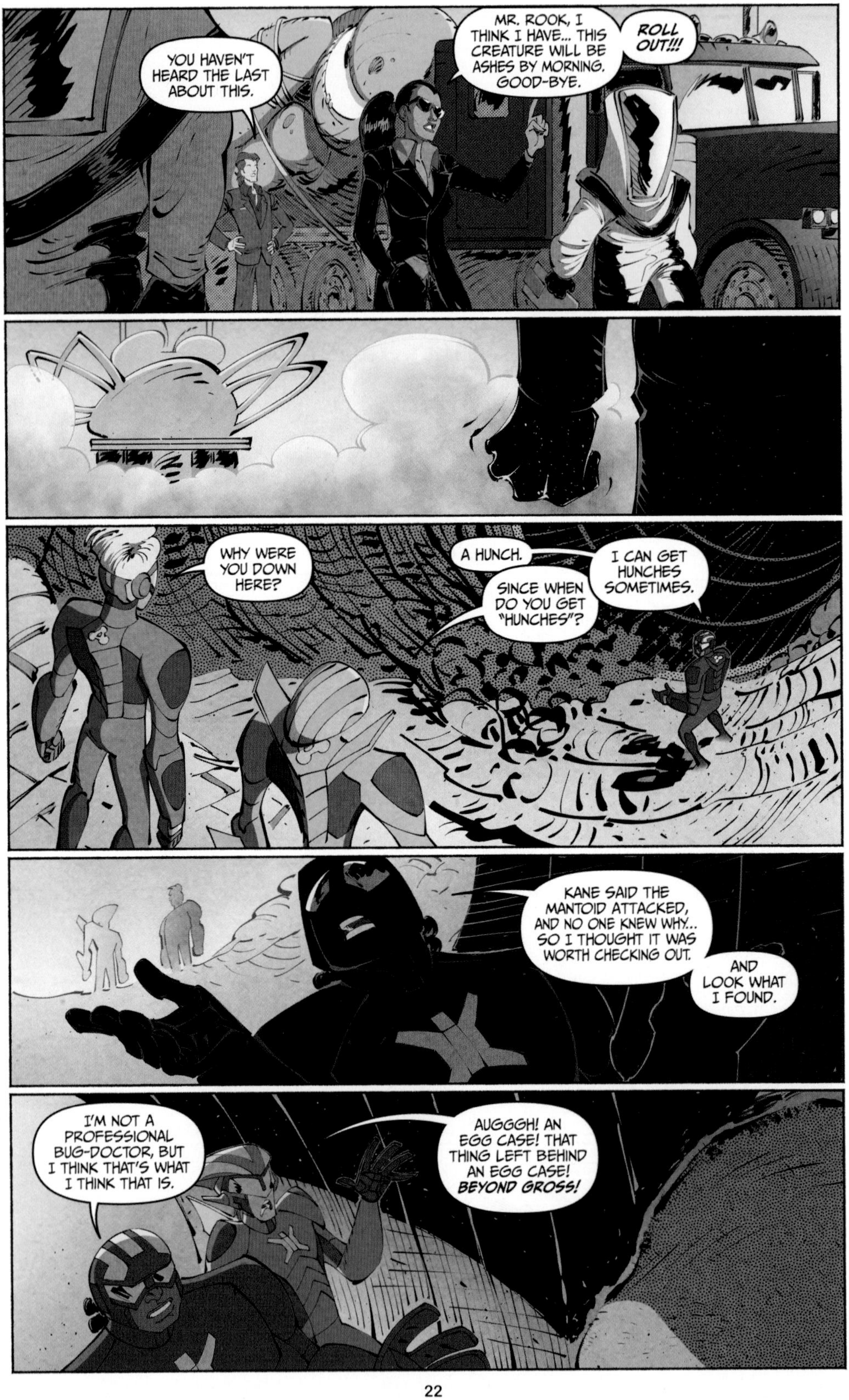
YOU HAVEN'T HEARD THE LAST ABOUT THIS.
MR. ROOK, I THINK I HAVE... THIS CREATURE WILL BE ASHES BY MORNING. GOOD-BYE.
ROLL OUT!!!
WHY WERE YOU DOWN HERE?
A HUNCH.
SINCE WHEN DO YOU GET "HUNCHES"?
I CAN GET HUNCHES SOMETIMES.
KANE SAID THE MANTOID ATTACKED, AND NO ONE KNEW WHY... SO I THOUGHT IT WAS WORTH CHECKING OUT.
AND LOOK WHAT I FOUND.
I'M NOT A PROFESSIONAL BUG-DOCTOR, BUT I THINK THAT'S WHAT I THINK THAT IS.
AUGGGH! AN EGG CASE! THAT THING LEFT BEHIND AN EGG CASE! BEYOND GROSS!

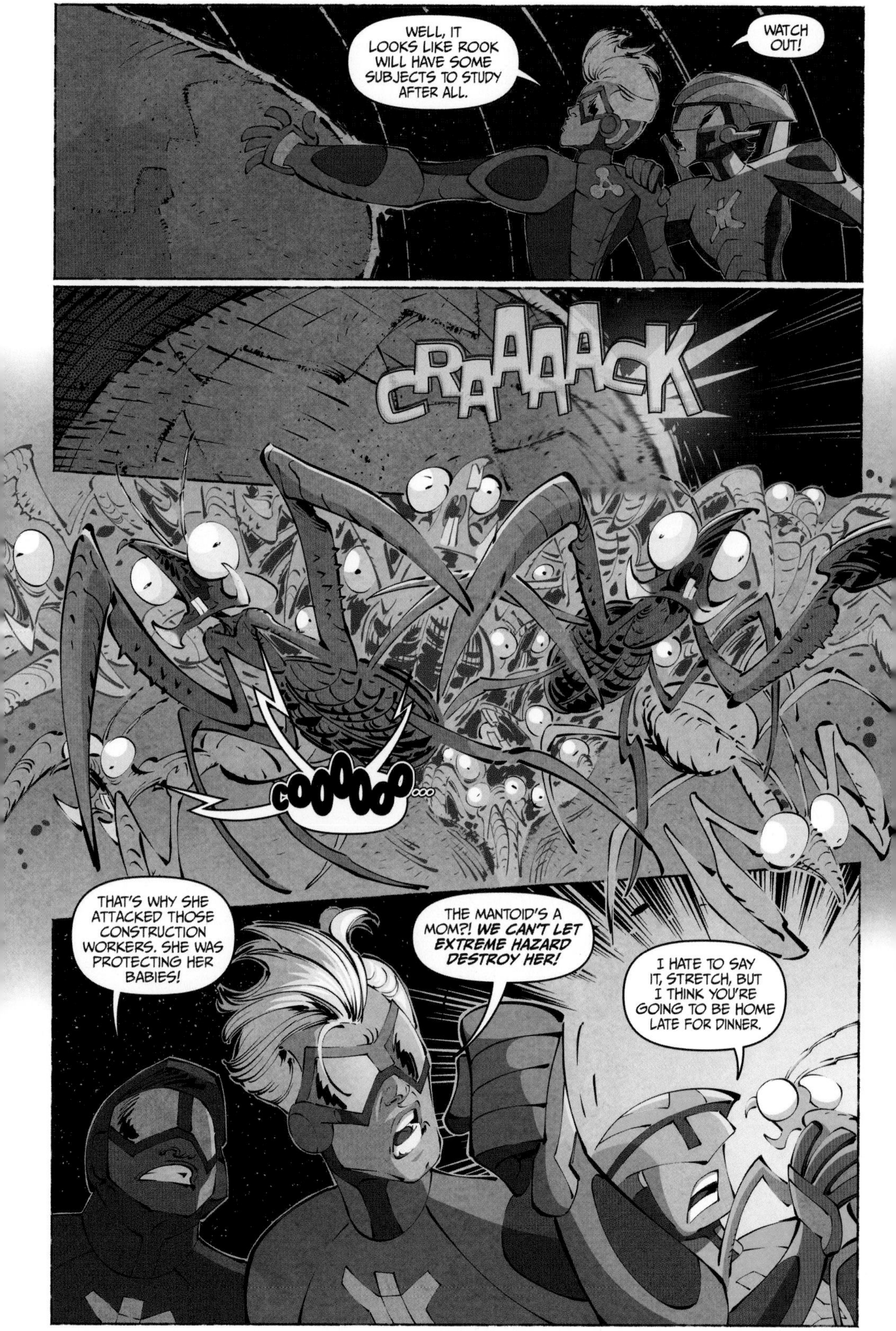
WELL, IT LOOKS LIKE ROOK WILL HAVE SOME SUBJECTS TO STUDY AFTER ALL.
WATCH OUT!
CRAAAACK
COOOOOOO...
THAT'S WHY SHE ATTACKED THOSE CONSTRUCTION WORKERS. SHE WAS PROTECTING HER BABIES!
THE MANTOID'S A MOM?! WE CAN'T LET EXTREME HAZARD DESTROY HER!
I HATE TO SAY IT, STRETCH, BUT I THINK YOU'RE GOING TO BE HOME LATE FOR DINNER.

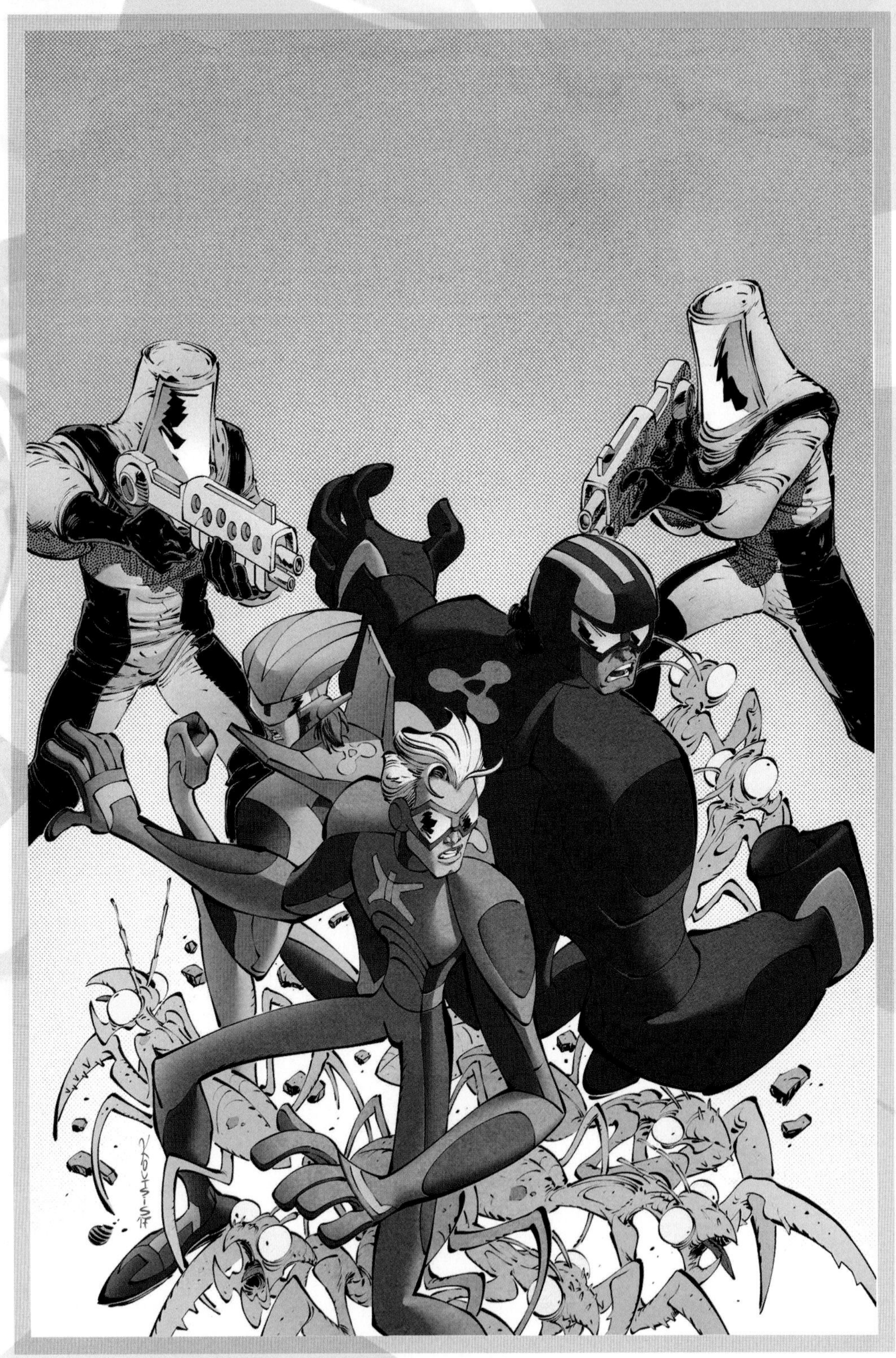

COVER ART
NIKOS KOUTSIS

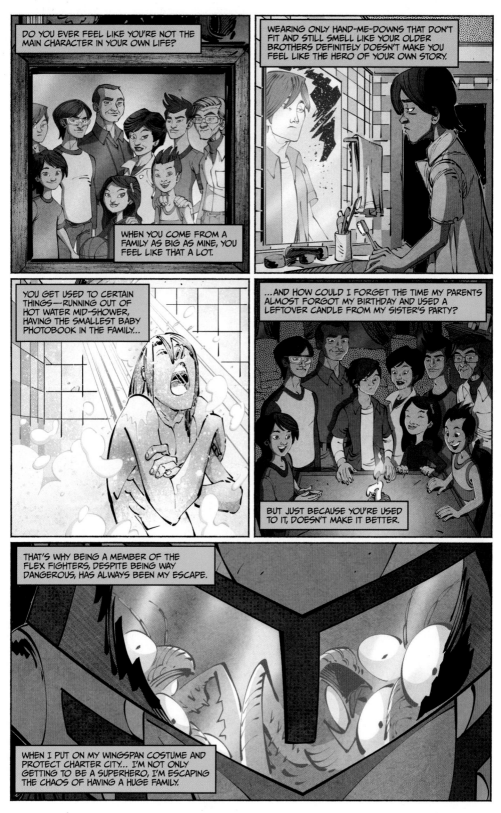

DO YOU EVER FEEL LIKE YOU'RE NOT THE MAIN CHARACTER IN YOUR OWN LIFE?

WHEN YOU COME FROM A FAMILY AS BIG AS MINE, YOU FEEL LIKE THAT A LOT.

WEARING ONLY HAND-ME-DOWNS THAT DON'T FIT AND STILL SMELL LIKE YOUR OLDER BROTHERS DEFINITELY DOESN'T MAKE YOU FEEL LIKE THE HERO OF YOUR OWN STORY.

YOU GET USED TO CERTAIN THINGS—RUNNING OUT OF HOT WATER MID-SHOWER, HAVING THE SMALLEST BABY PHOTOBOOK IN THE FAMILY...

...AND HOW COULD I FORGET THE TIME MY PARENTS ALMOST FORGOT MY BIRTHDAY AND USED A LEFTOVER CANDLE FROM MY SISTER'S PARTY?

BUT JUST BECAUSE YOU'RE USED TO IT, DOESN'T MAKE IT BETTER.

THAT'S WHY BEING A MEMBER OF THE FLEX FIGHTERS, DESPITE BEING WAY DANGEROUS, HAS ALWAYS BEEN MY ESCAPE.

WHEN I PUT ON MY WINGSPAN COSTUME AND PROTECT CHARTER CITY... I'M NOT ONLY GETTING TO BE A SUPERHERO, I'M ESCAPING THE CHAOS OF HAVING A HUGE FAMILY.

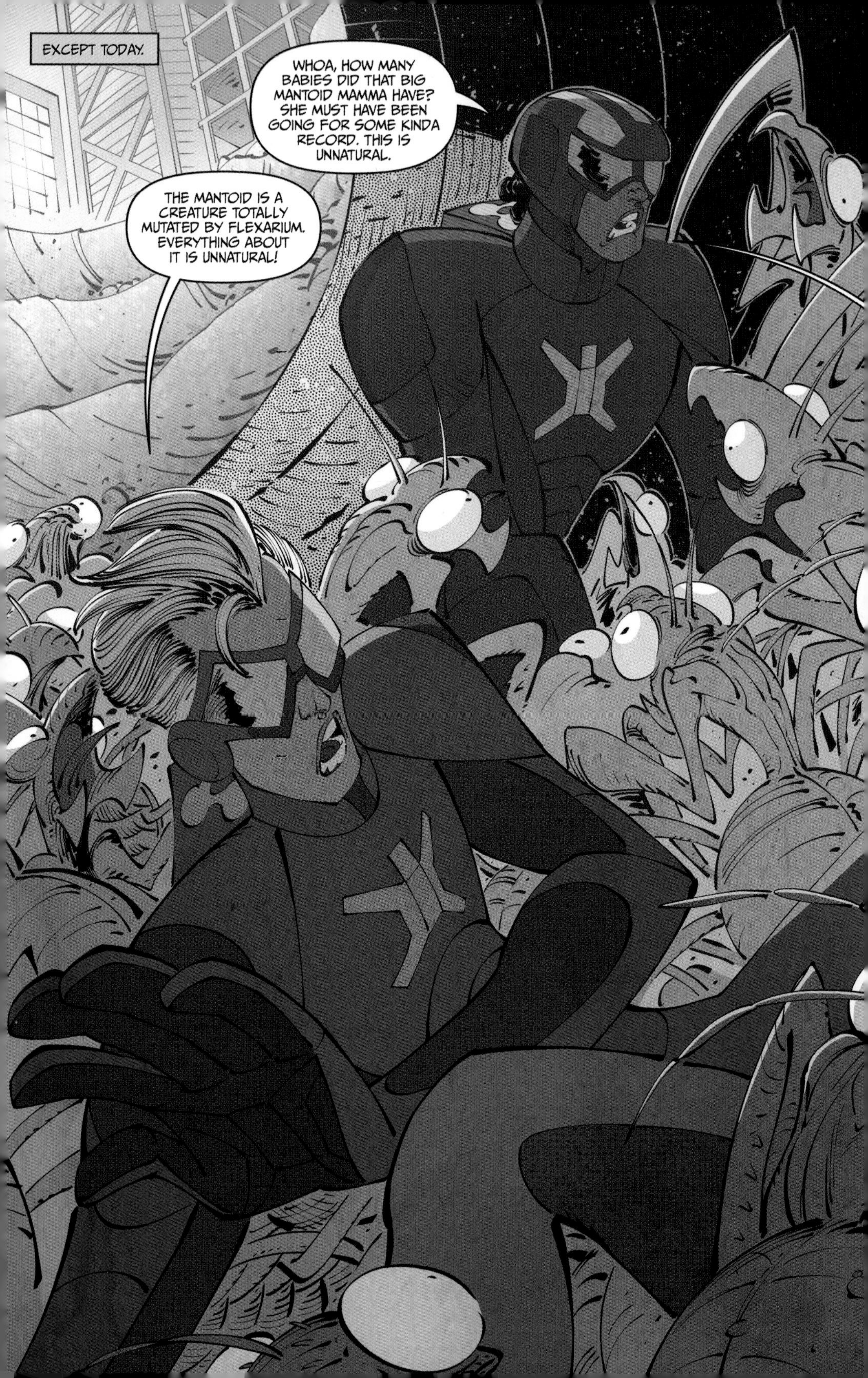
EXCEPT TODAY.
WHOA, HOW MANY BABIES DID THAT BIG MANTOID MAMMA HAVE? SHE MUST HAVE BEEN GOING FOR SOME KINDA RECORD. THIS IS UNNATURAL.
THE MANTOID IS A CREATURE TOTALLY MUTATED BY FLEXARIUM. EVERYTHING ABOUT IT IS UNNATURAL!

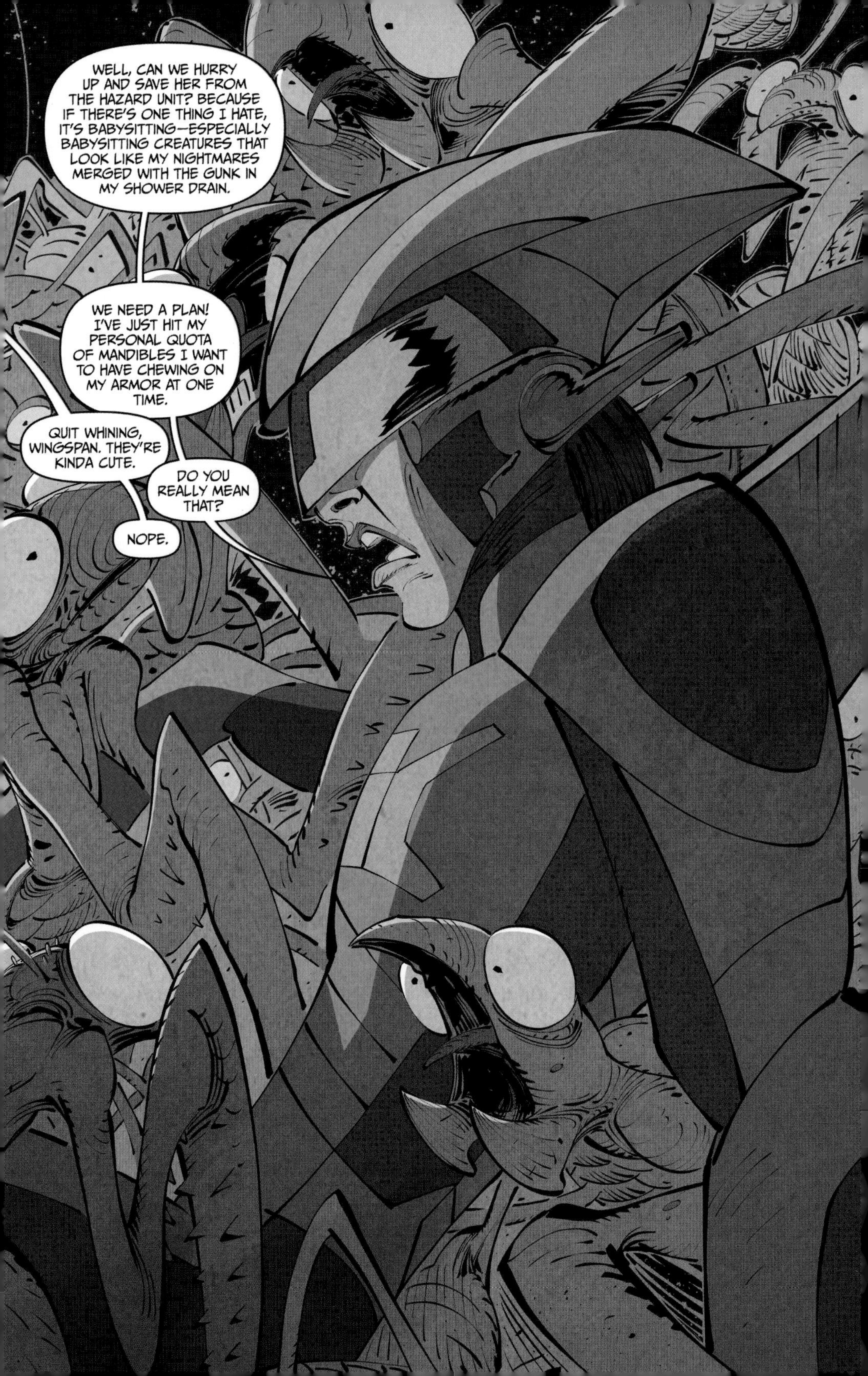
WELL, CAN WE HURRY UP AND SAVE HER FROM THE HAZARD UNIT? BECAUSE IF THERE'S ONE THING I HATE, IT'S BABYSITTING—ESPECIALLY BABYSITTING CREATURES THAT LOOK LIKE MY NIGHTMARES MERGED WITH THE GUNK IN MY SHOWER DRAIN.
WE NEED A PLAN! I'VE JUST HIT MY PERSONAL QUOTA OF MANDIBLES I WANT TO HAVE CHEWING ON MY ARMOR AT ONE TIME.
QUIT WHINING, WINGSPAN. THEY'RE KINDA CUTE.
DO YOU REALLY MEAN THAT?
NOPE.

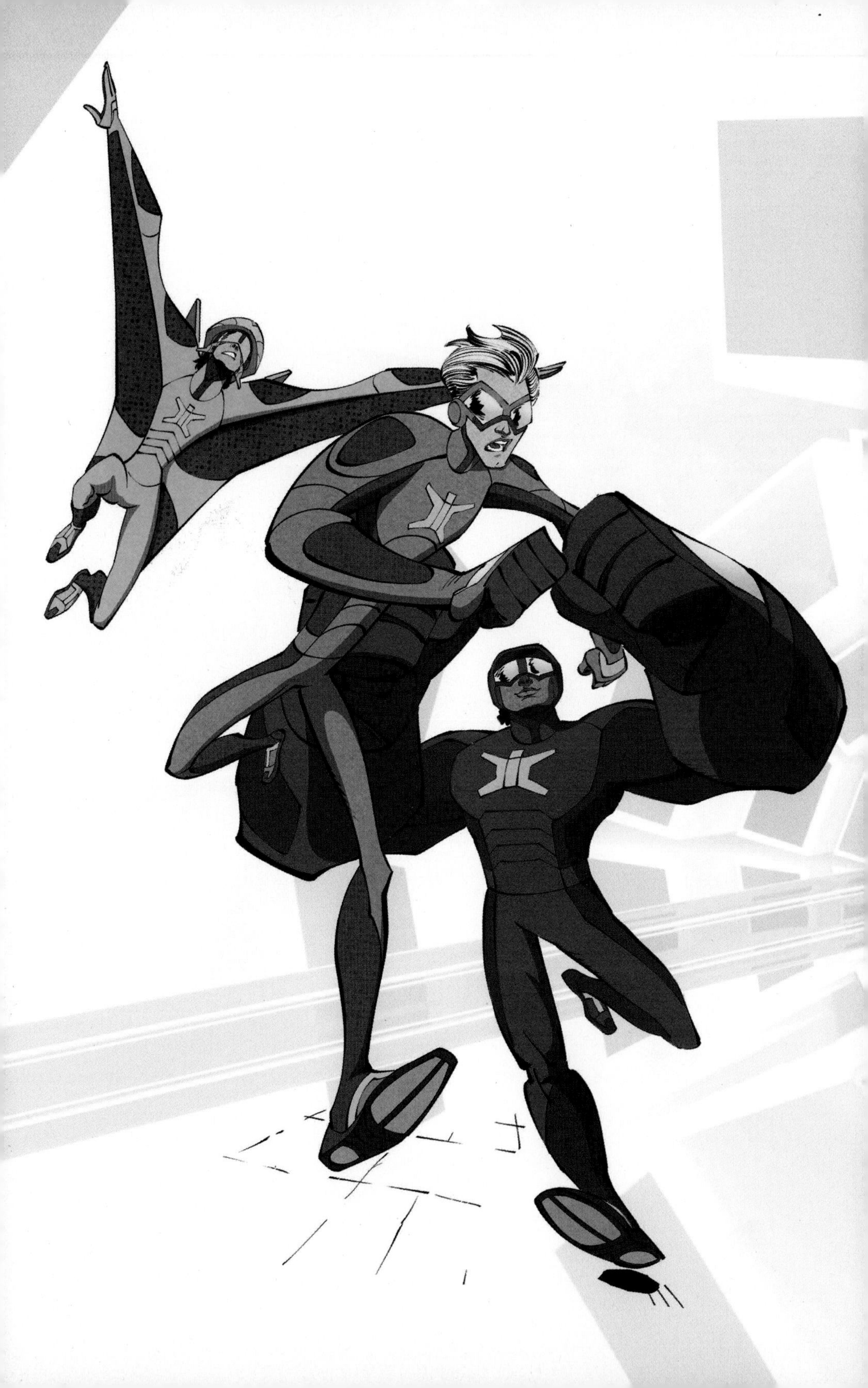

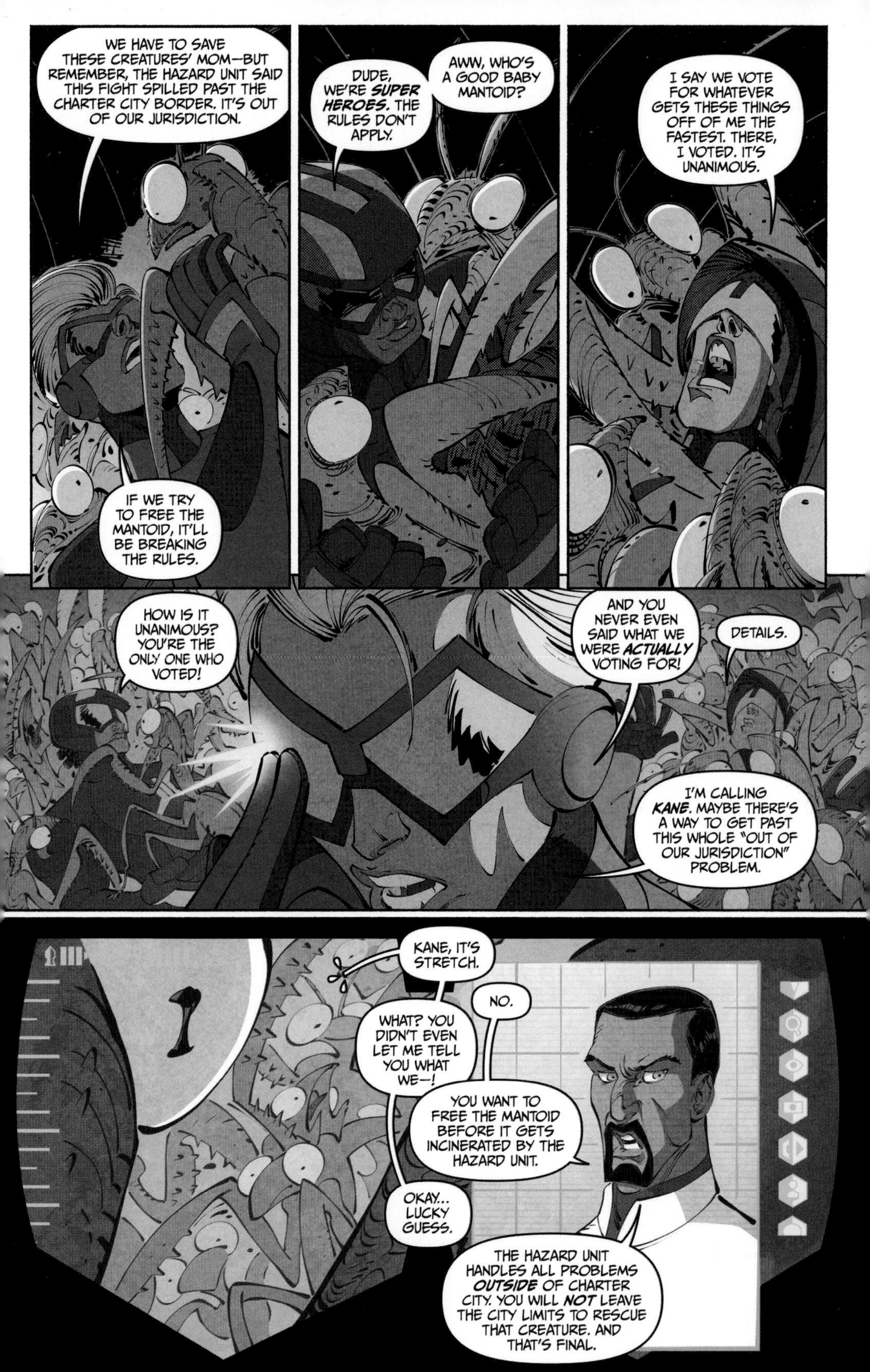
WE HAVE TO SAVE THESE CREATURES' MOM—BUT REMEMBER, THE HAZARD UNIT SAID THIS FIGHT SPILLED PAST THE CHARTER CITY BORDER. IT'S OUT OF OUR JURISDICTION.
IF WE TRY TO FREE THE MANTOID, IT'LL BE BREAKING THE RULES.
AWW, WHO'S A GOOD BABY MANTOID?
DUDE, WE'RE SUPER HEROES. THE RULES DON'T APPLY.
I SAY WE VOTE FOR WHATEVER GETS THESE THINGS OFF OF ME THE FASTEST. THERE, I VOTED. IT'S UNANIMOUS.
HOW IS IT UNANIMOUS? YOU'RE THE ONLY ONE WHO VOTED!
AND YOU NEVER EVEN SAID WHAT WE WERE ACTUALLY VOTING FOR!
DETAILS.
I'M CALLING KANE. MAYBE THERE'S A WAY TO GET PAST THIS WHOLE "OUT OF OUR JURISDICTION" PROBLEM.
KANE, IT'S STRETCH.
NO.
WHAT? YOU DIDN'T EVEN LET ME TELL YOU WHAT WE—!
YOU WANT TO FREE THE MANTOID BEFORE IT GETS INCINERATED BY THE HAZARD UNIT.
OKAY... LUCKY GUESS.
THE HAZARD UNIT HANDLES ALL PROBLEMS OUTSIDE OF CHARTER CITY. YOU WILL NOT LEAVE THE CITY LIMITS TO RESCUE THAT CREATURE. AND THAT'S FINAL.

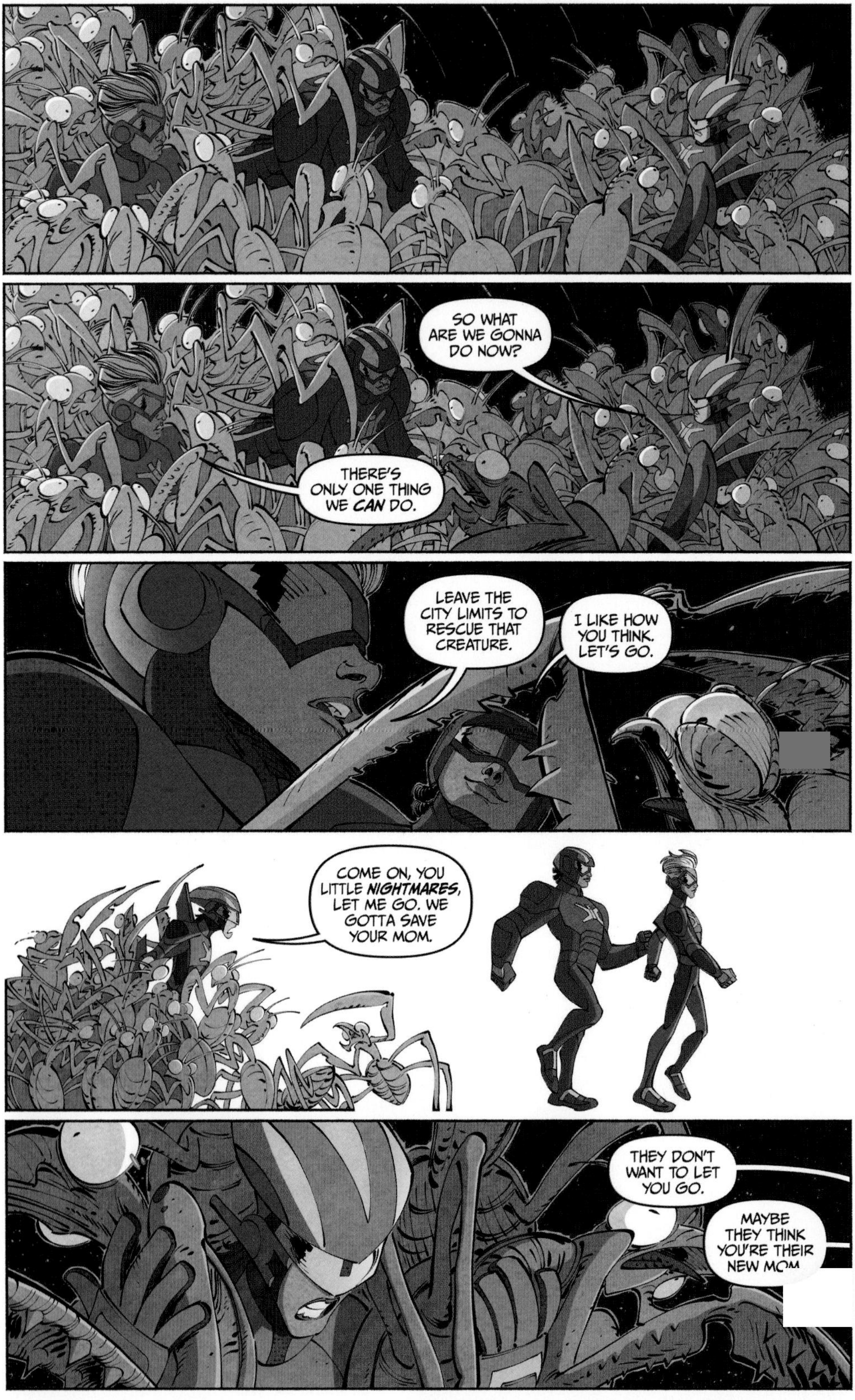

SO WHAT ARE WE GONNA DO NOW?
THERE'S ONLY ONE THING WE **CAN** DO.
LEAVE THE CITY LIMITS TO RESCUE THAT CREATURE.
I LIKE HOW YOU THINK. LET'S GO.
COME ON, YOU LITTLE **NIGHTMARES**, LET ME GO. WE GOTTA SAVE YOUR MOM.
THEY DON'T WANT TO LET YOU GO.
MAYBE THEY THINK YOU'RE THEIR NEW MOM

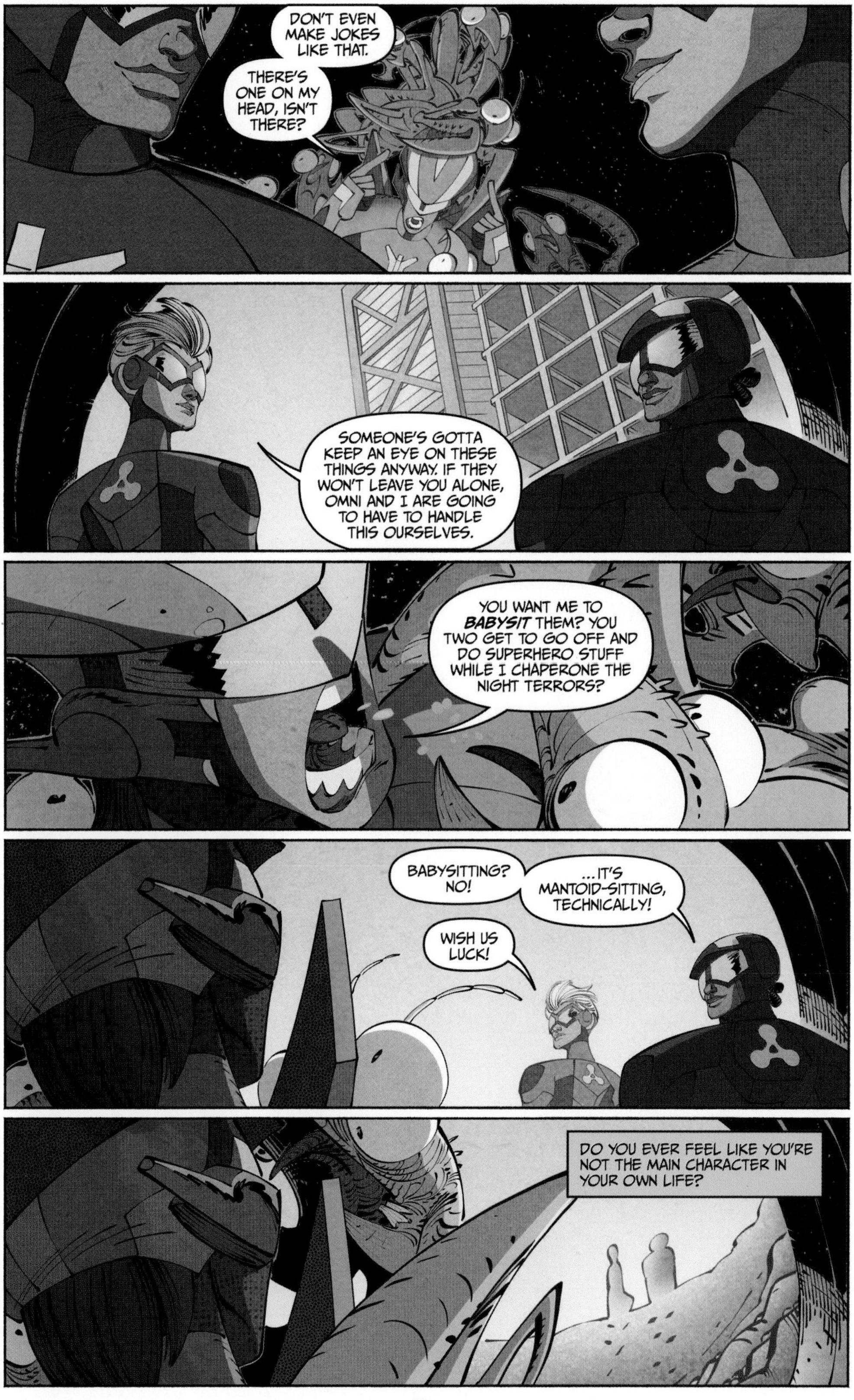
DON'T EVEN MAKE JOKES LIKE THAT.
THERE'S ONE ON MY HEAD, ISN'T THERE?
SOMEONE'S GOTTA KEEP AN EYE ON THESE THINGS ANYWAY. IF THEY WON'T LEAVE YOU ALONE, OMNI AND I ARE GOING TO HAVE TO HANDLE THIS OURSELVES.
YOU WANT ME TO *BABYSIT* THEM? YOU TWO GET TO GO OFF AND DO SUPERHERO STUFF WHILE I CHAPERONE THE NIGHT TERRORS?
BABYSITTING? NO!
...IT'S MANTOID-SITTING, TECHNICALLY!
WISH US LUCK!
DO YOU EVER FEEL LIKE YOU'RE NOT THE MAIN CHARACTER IN YOUR OWN LIFE?

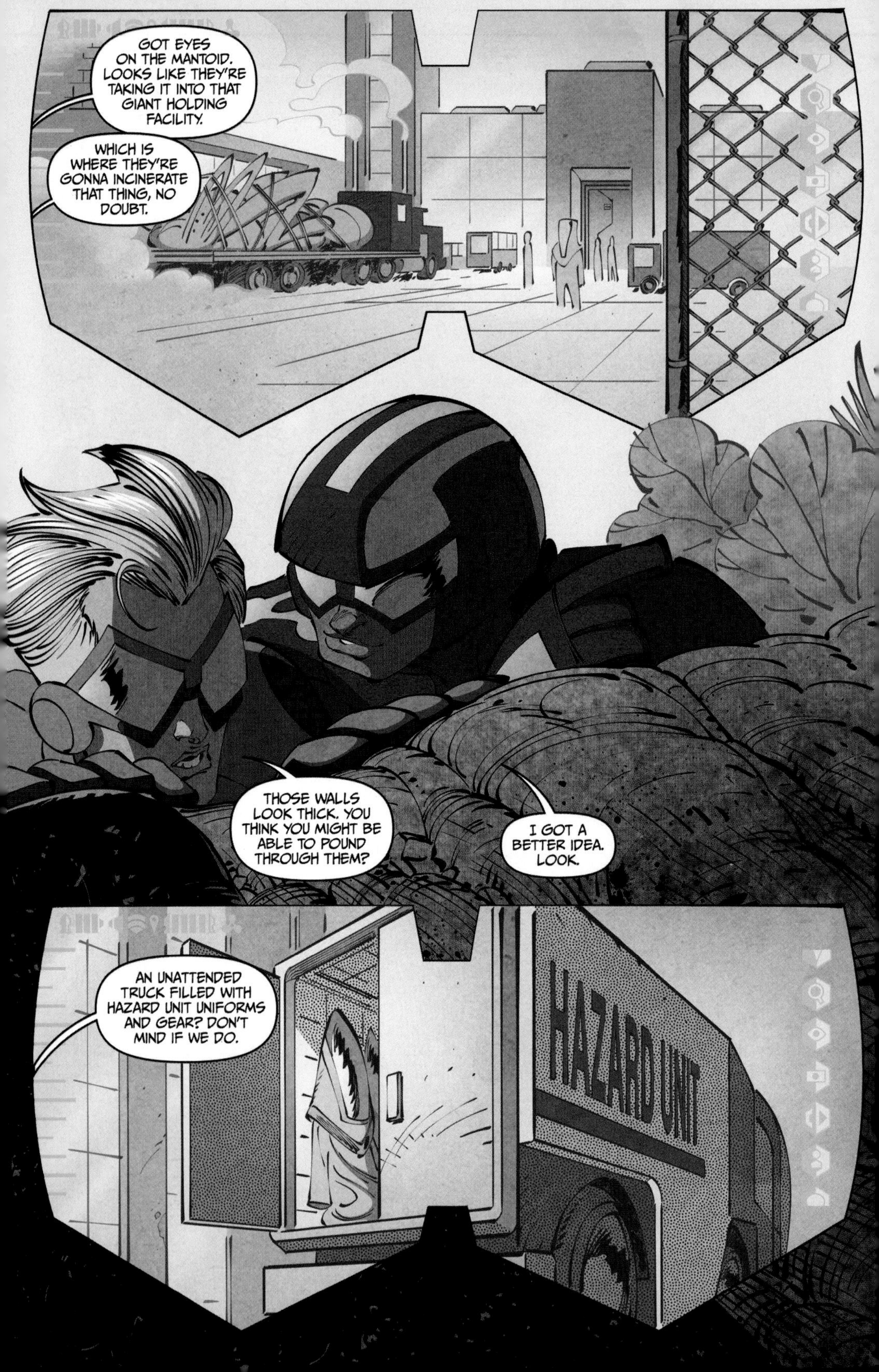
GOT EYES ON THE MANTOID. LOOKS LIKE THEY'RE TAKING IT INTO THAT GIANT HOLDING FACILITY.
WHICH IS WHERE THEY'RE GONNA INCINERATE THAT THING, NO DOUBT.
THOSE WALLS LOOK THICK. YOU THINK YOU MIGHT BE ABLE TO POUND THROUGH THEM?
I GOT A BETTER IDEA. LOOK.
AN UNATTENDED TRUCK FILLED WITH HAZARD UNIT UNIFORMS AND GEAR? DON'T MIND IF WE DO.
HAZARD UNIT

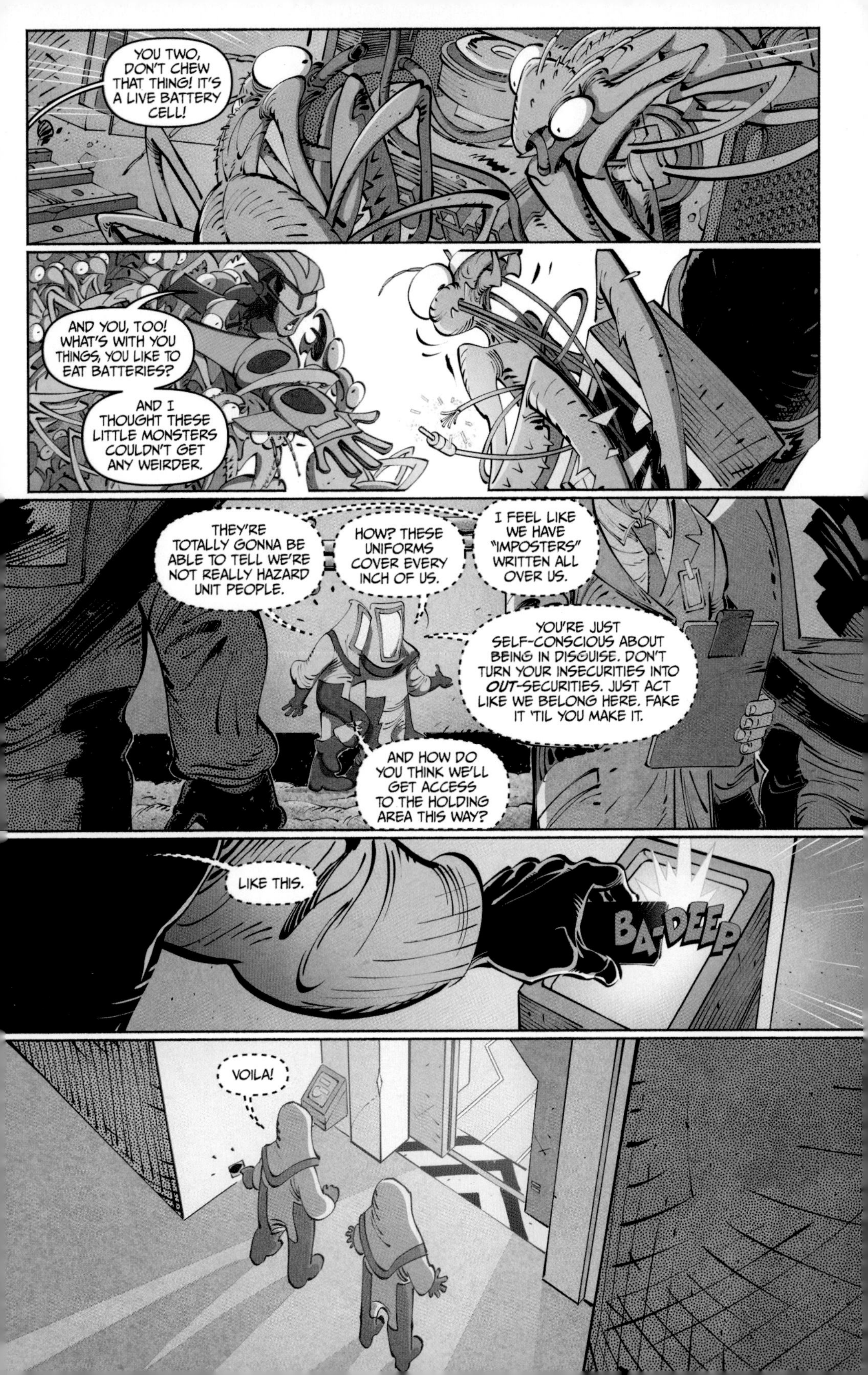
YOU TWO, DON'T CHEW THAT THING! IT'S A LIVE BATTERY CELL!
AND YOU, TOO! WHAT'S WITH YOU THINGS, YOU LIKE TO EAT BATTERIES?
AND I THOUGHT THESE LITTLE MONSTERS COULDN'T GET ANY WEIRDER.
THEY'RE TOTALLY GONNA BE ABLE TO TELL WE'RE NOT REALLY HAZARD UNIT PEOPLE.
HOW? THESE UNIFORMS COVER EVERY INCH OF US.
I FEEL LIKE WE HAVE "IMPOSTERS" WRITTEN ALL OVER US.
YOU'RE JUST SELF-CONSCIOUS ABOUT BEING IN DISGUISE. DON'T TURN YOUR INSECURITIES INTO *OUT*-SECURITIES. JUST ACT LIKE WE BELONG HERE. FAKE IT 'TIL YOU MAKE IT.
AND HOW DO YOU THINK WE'LL GET ACCESS TO THE HOLDING AREA THIS WAY?
LIKE THIS.
BA-DEEP
VOILA!

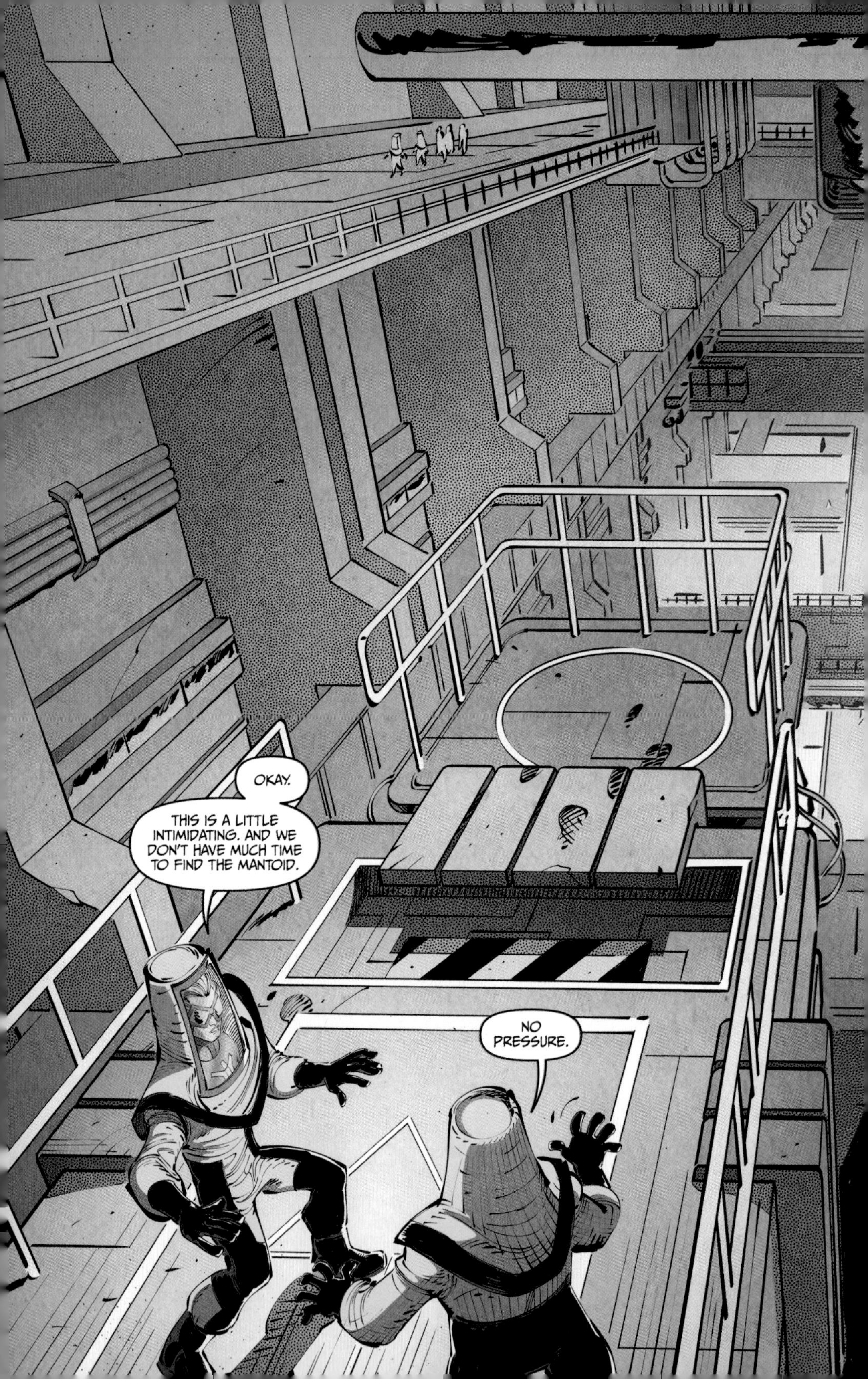
OKAY.
THIS IS A LITTLE INTIMIDATING. AND WE DON'T HAVE MUCH TIME TO FIND THE MANTOID.
NO PRESSURE.

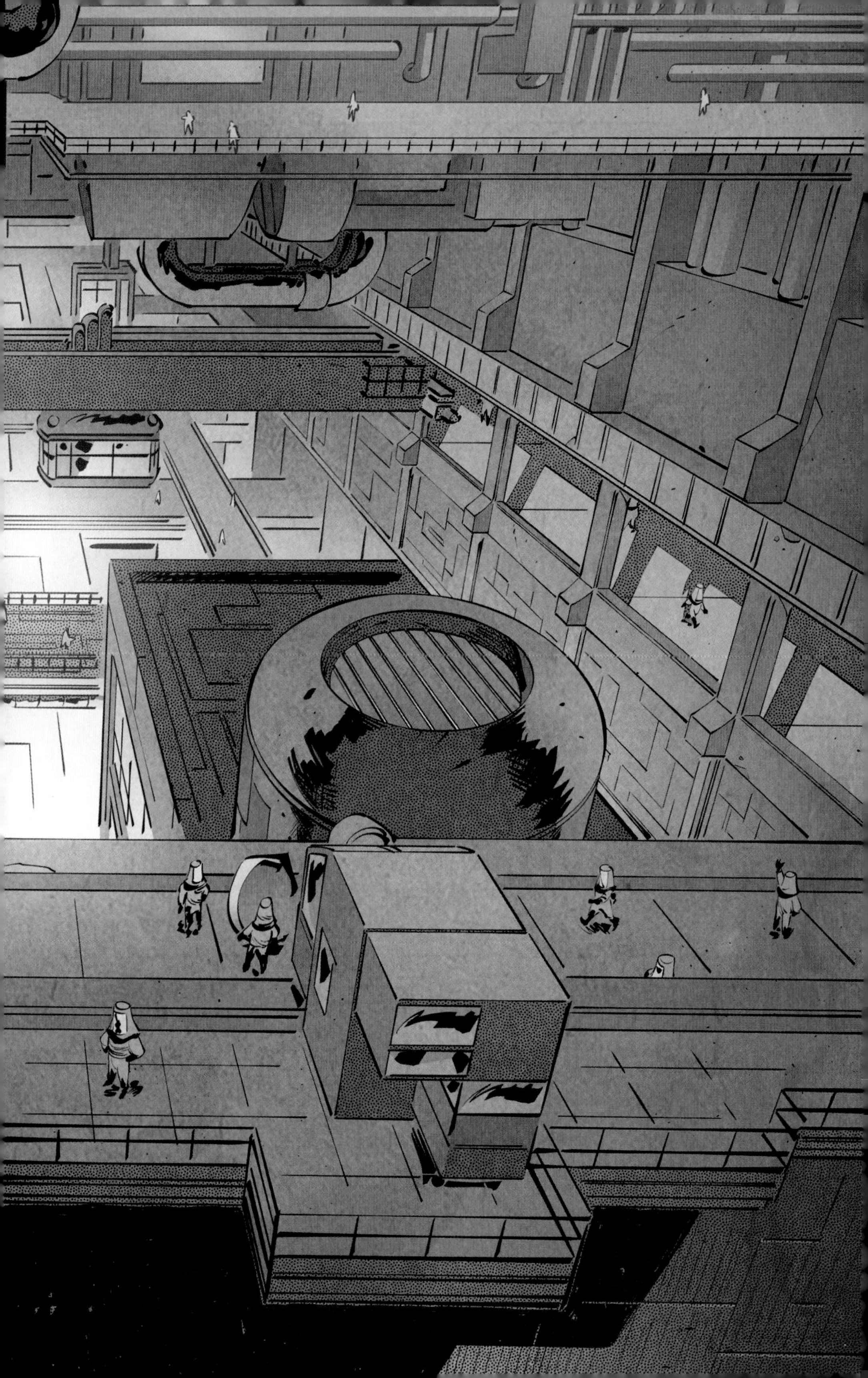

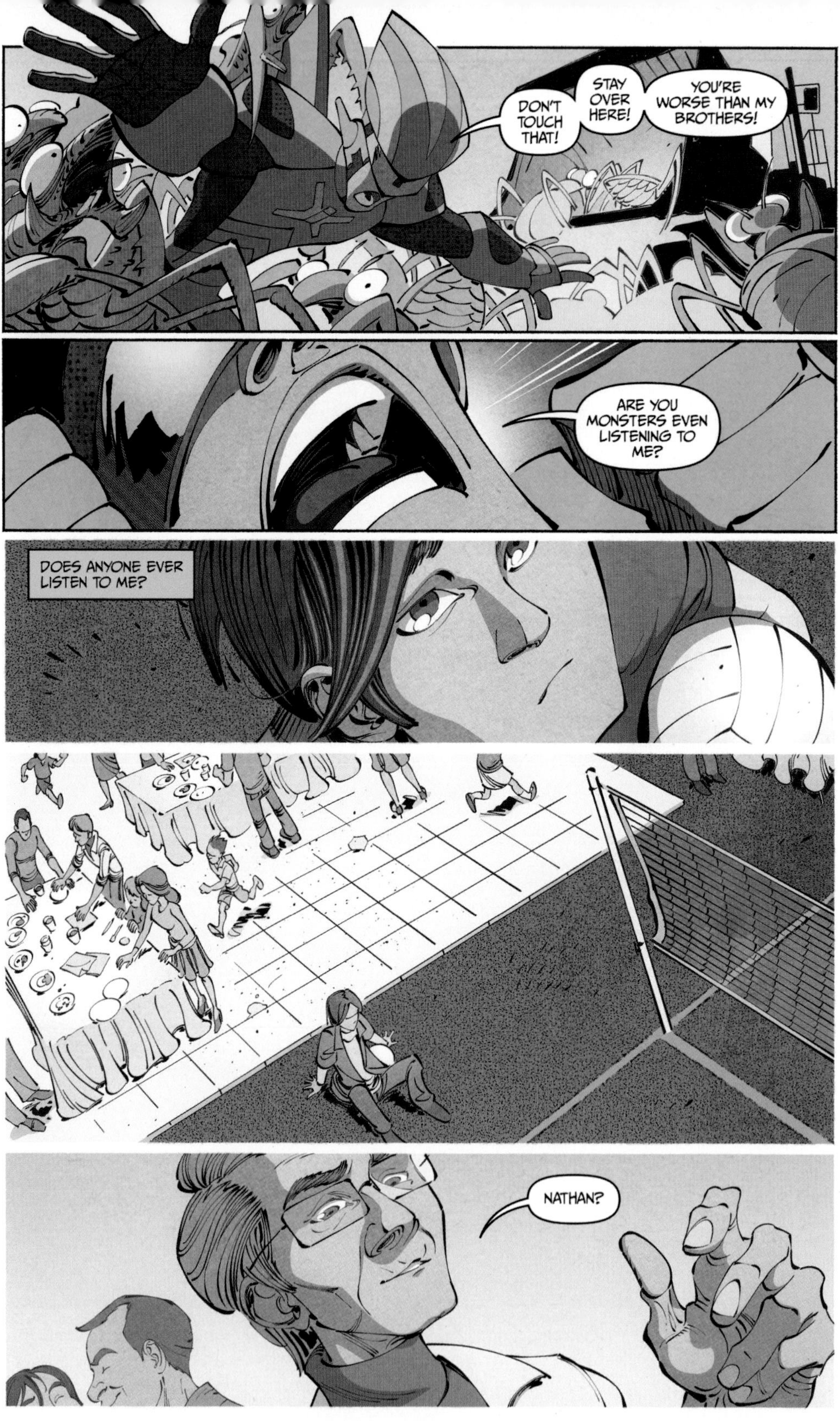
DON'T TOUCH THAT!
STAY OVER HERE!
YOU'RE WORSE THAN MY BROTHERS!
ARE YOU MONSTERS EVEN LISTENING TO ME?
DOES ANYONE EVER LISTEN TO ME?
NATHAN?

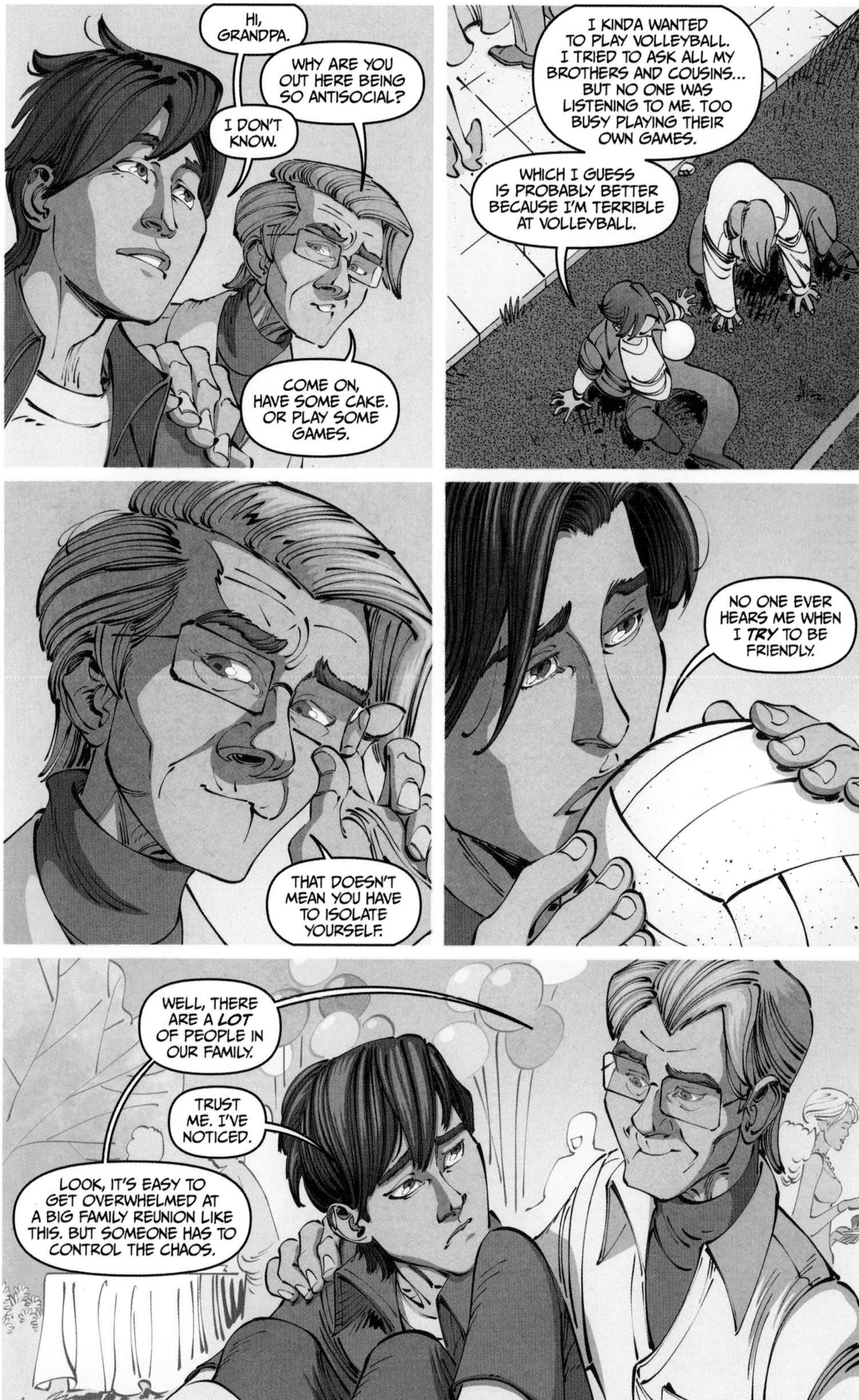
HI, GRANDPA.
WHY ARE YOU OUT HERE BEING SO ANTISOCIAL?
I DON'T KNOW.
COME ON, HAVE SOME CAKE. OR PLAY SOME GAMES.
I KINDA WANTED TO PLAY VOLLEYBALL. I TRIED TO ASK ALL MY BROTHERS AND COUSINS... BUT NO ONE WAS LISTENING TO ME. TOO BUSY PLAYING THEIR OWN GAMES.
WHICH I GUESS IS PROBABLY BETTER BECAUSE I'M TERRIBLE AT VOLLEYBALL.
THAT DOESN'T MEAN YOU HAVE TO ISOLATE YOURSELF.
NO ONE EVER HEARS ME WHEN I *TRY* TO BE FRIENDLY.
WELL, THERE ARE A *LOT* OF PEOPLE IN OUR FAMILY.
TRUST ME. I'VE NOTICED.
LOOK, IT'S EASY TO GET OVERWHELMED AT A BIG FAMILY REUNION LIKE THIS. BUT SOMEONE HAS TO CONTROL THE CHAOS.

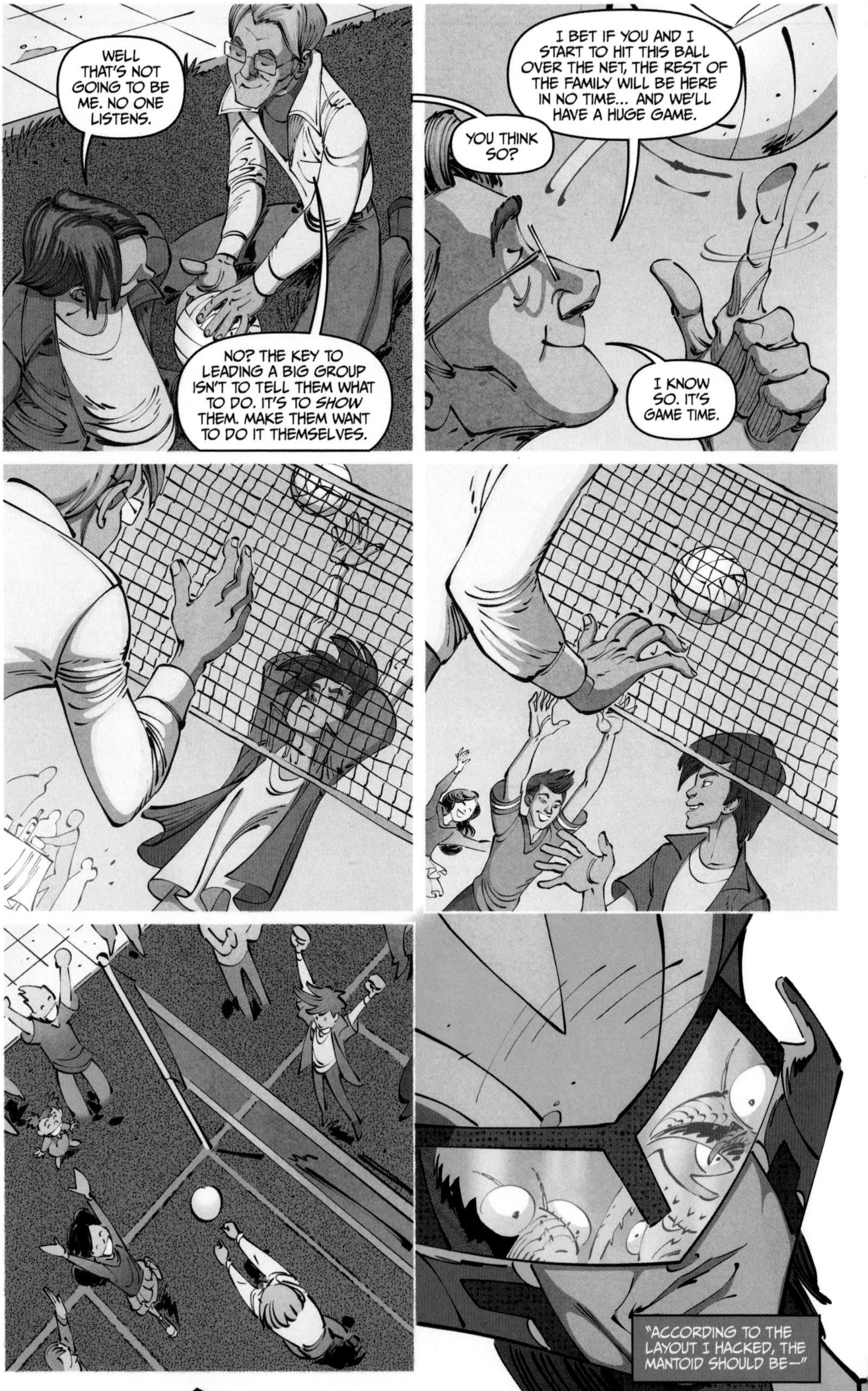
WELL THAT'S NOT GOING TO BE ME. NO ONE LISTENS.
NO? THE KEY TO LEADING A BIG GROUP ISN'T TO TELL THEM WHAT TO DO. IT'S TO *SHOW* THEM. MAKE THEM WANT TO DO IT THEMSELVES.
I BET IF YOU AND I START TO HIT THIS BALL OVER THE NET, THE REST OF THE FAMILY WILL BE HERE IN NO TIME... AND WE'LL HAVE A HUGE GAME.
YOU THINK SO?
I KNOW SO. IT'S GAME TIME.
"ACCORDING TO THE LAYOUT I HACKED, THE MANTOID SHOULD BE—"

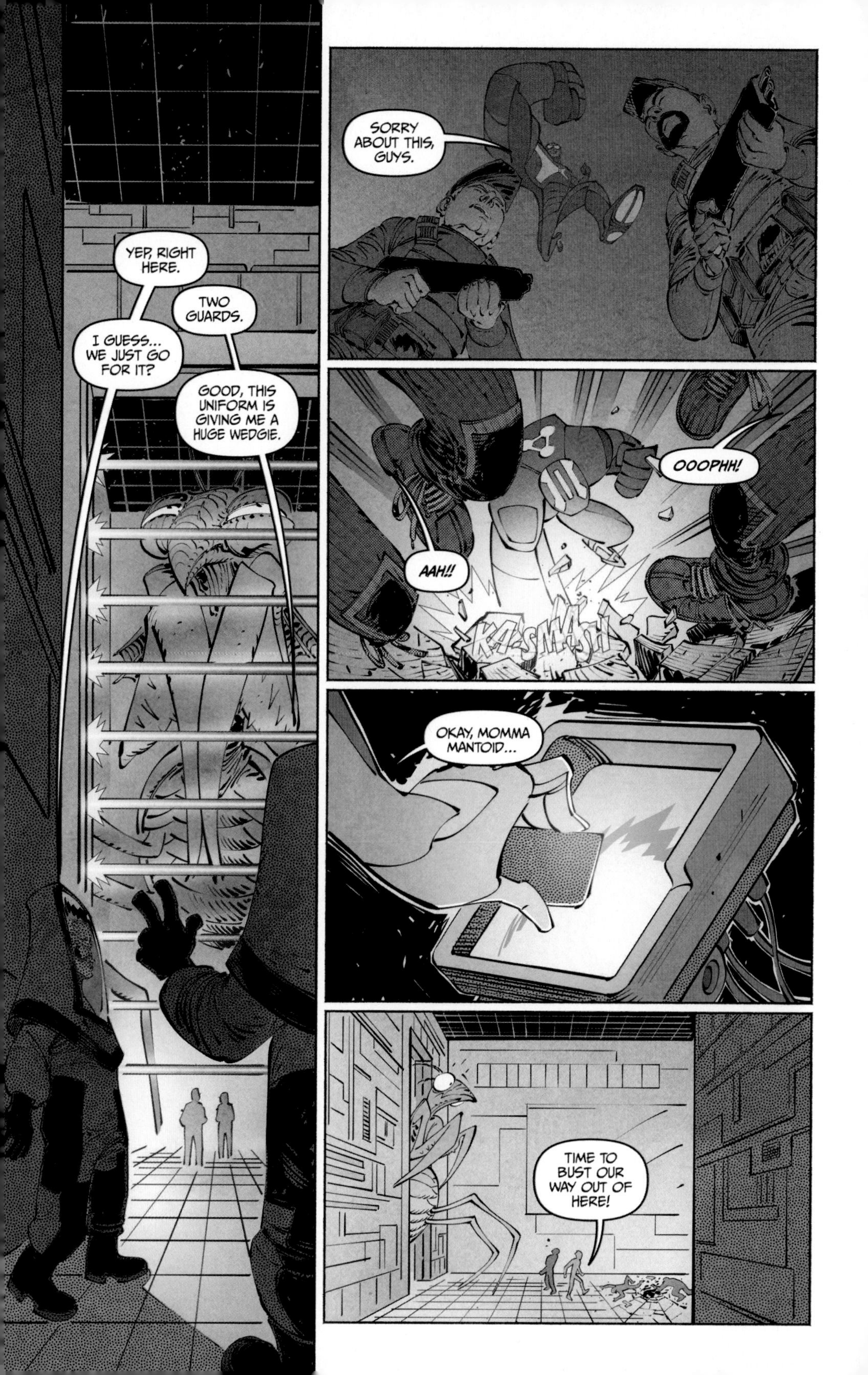
YEP, RIGHT HERE.
TWO GUARDS.
I GUESS... WE JUST GO FOR IT?
GOOD, THIS UNIFORM IS GIVING ME A HUGE WEDGIE.
SORRY ABOUT THIS, GUYS.
OOOPHH!
AAH!!
KA-SMASH!
OKAY, MOMMA MANTOID...
TIME TO BUST OUR WAY OUT OF HERE!

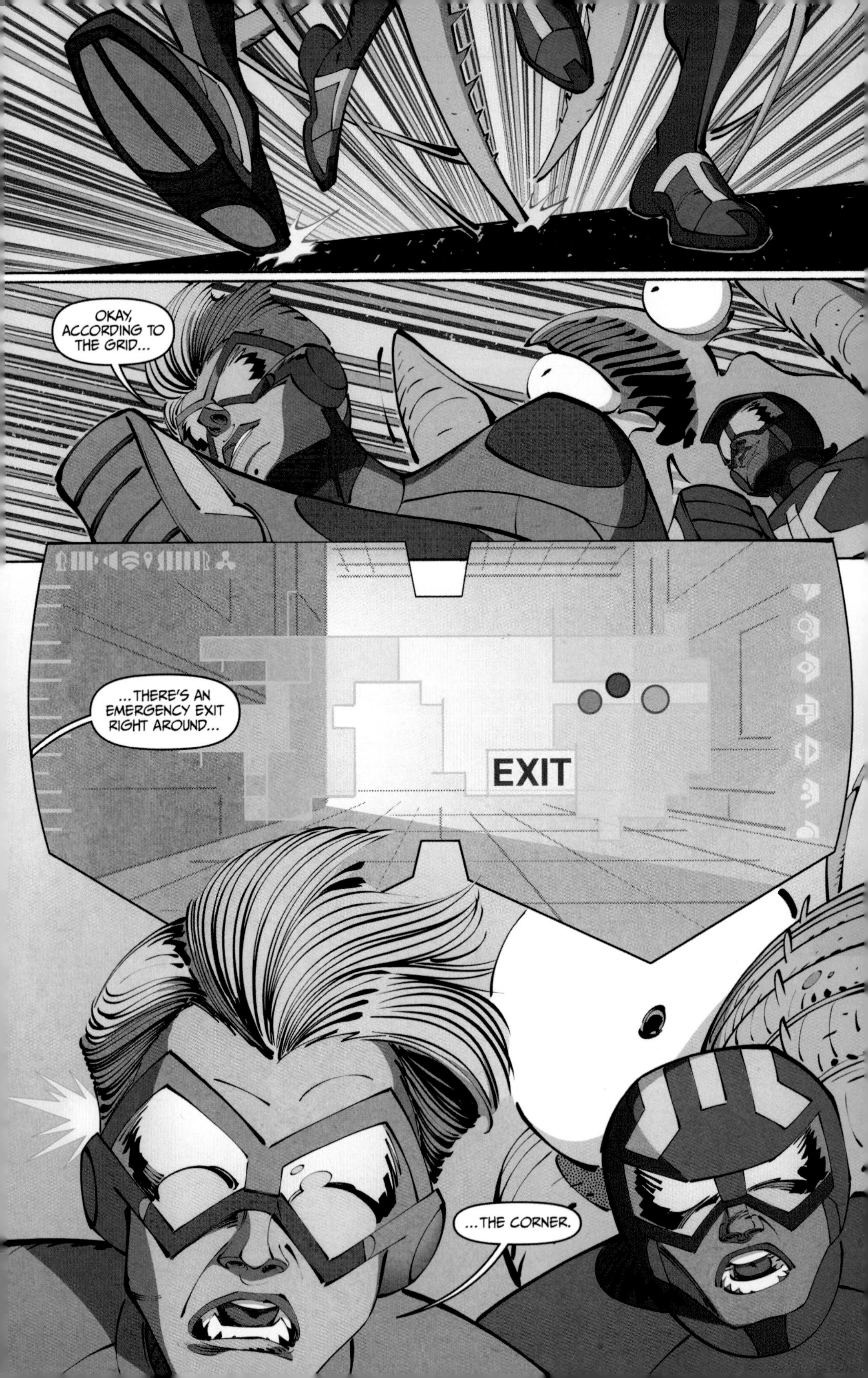
OKAY, ACCORDING TO THE GRID...
...THERE'S AN EMERGENCY EXIT RIGHT AROUND...
EXIT
...THE CORNER.

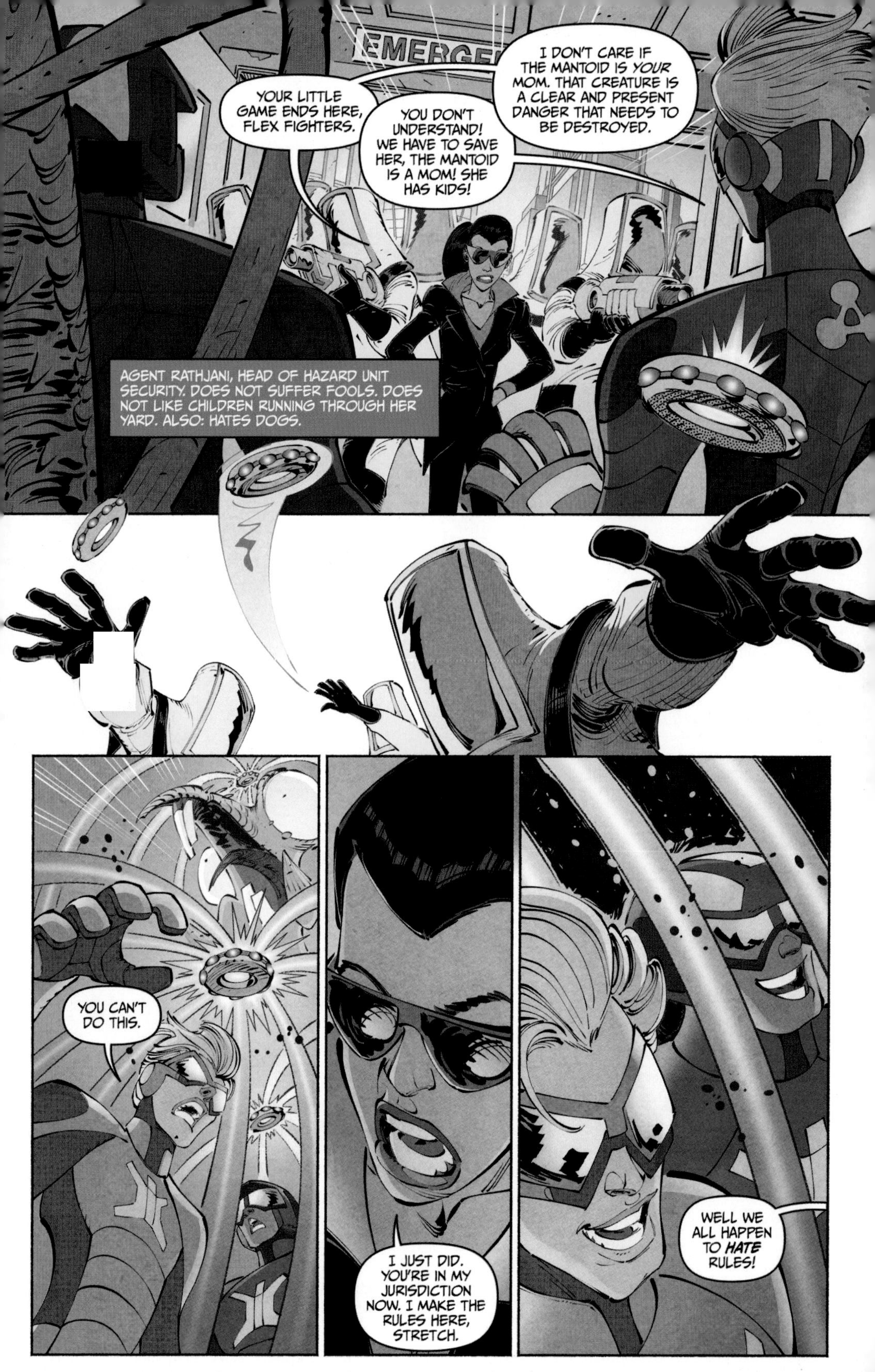
EMERGE
YOUR LITTLE GAME ENDS HERE, FLEX FIGHTERS.
YOU DON'T UNDERSTAND! WE HAVE TO SAVE HER, THE MANTOID IS A MOM! SHE HAS KIDS!
I DON'T CARE IF THE MANTOID IS *YOUR* MOM. THAT CREATURE IS A CLEAR AND PRESENT DANGER THAT NEEDS TO BE DESTROYED.
AGENT RATHJANI, HEAD OF HAZARD UNIT SECURITY. DOES NOT SUFFER FOOLS. DOES NOT LIKE CHILDREN RUNNING THROUGH HER YARD. ALSO: HATES DOGS.
YOU CAN'T DO THIS.
I JUST DID. YOU'RE IN MY JURISDICTION NOW. I MAKE THE RULES HERE, STRETCH.
WELL WE ALL HAPPEN TO ***HATE*** RULES!

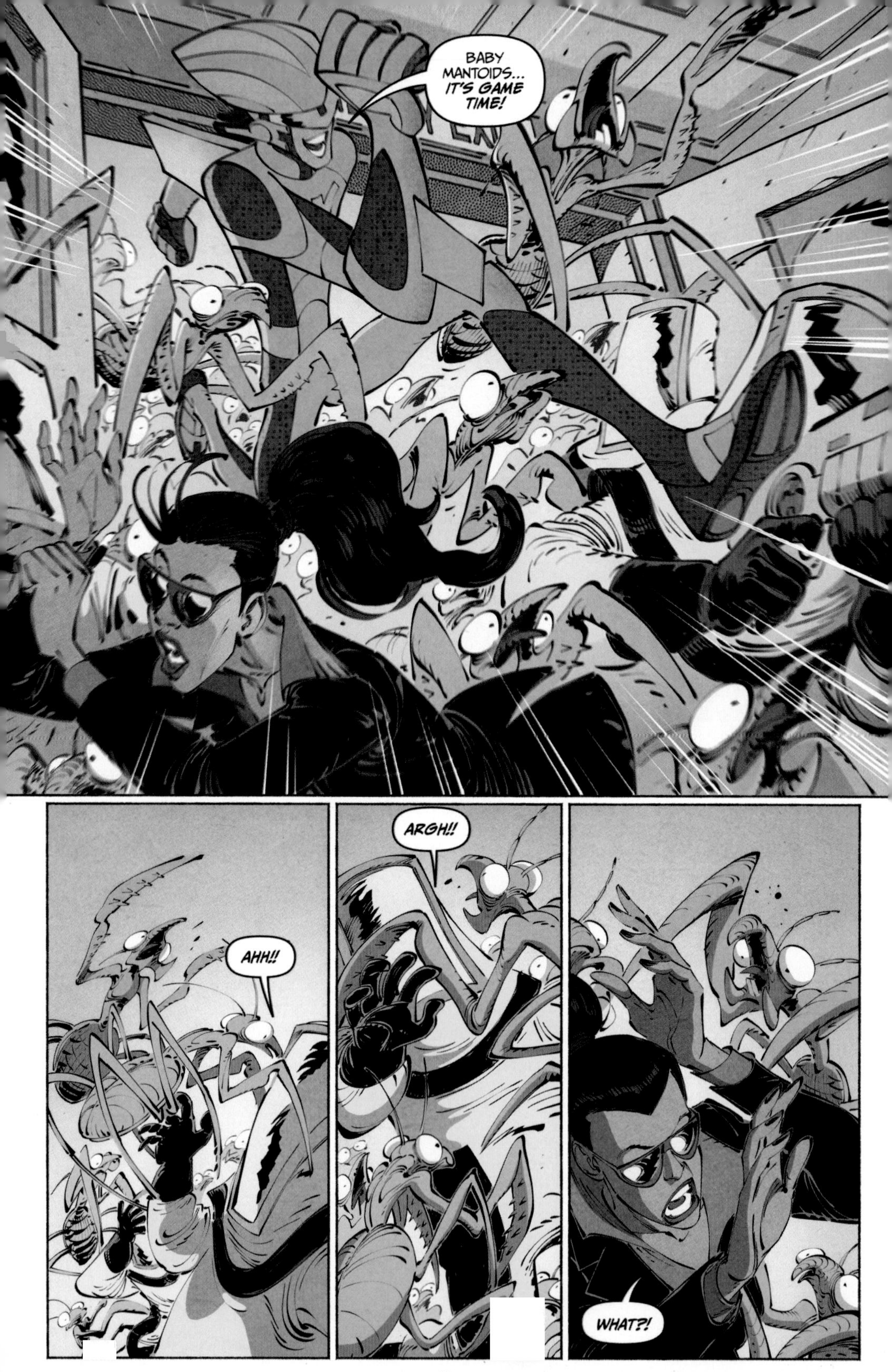
BABY MANTOIDS... IT'S GAME TIME!
AHH!!
ARGH!!
WHAT?!

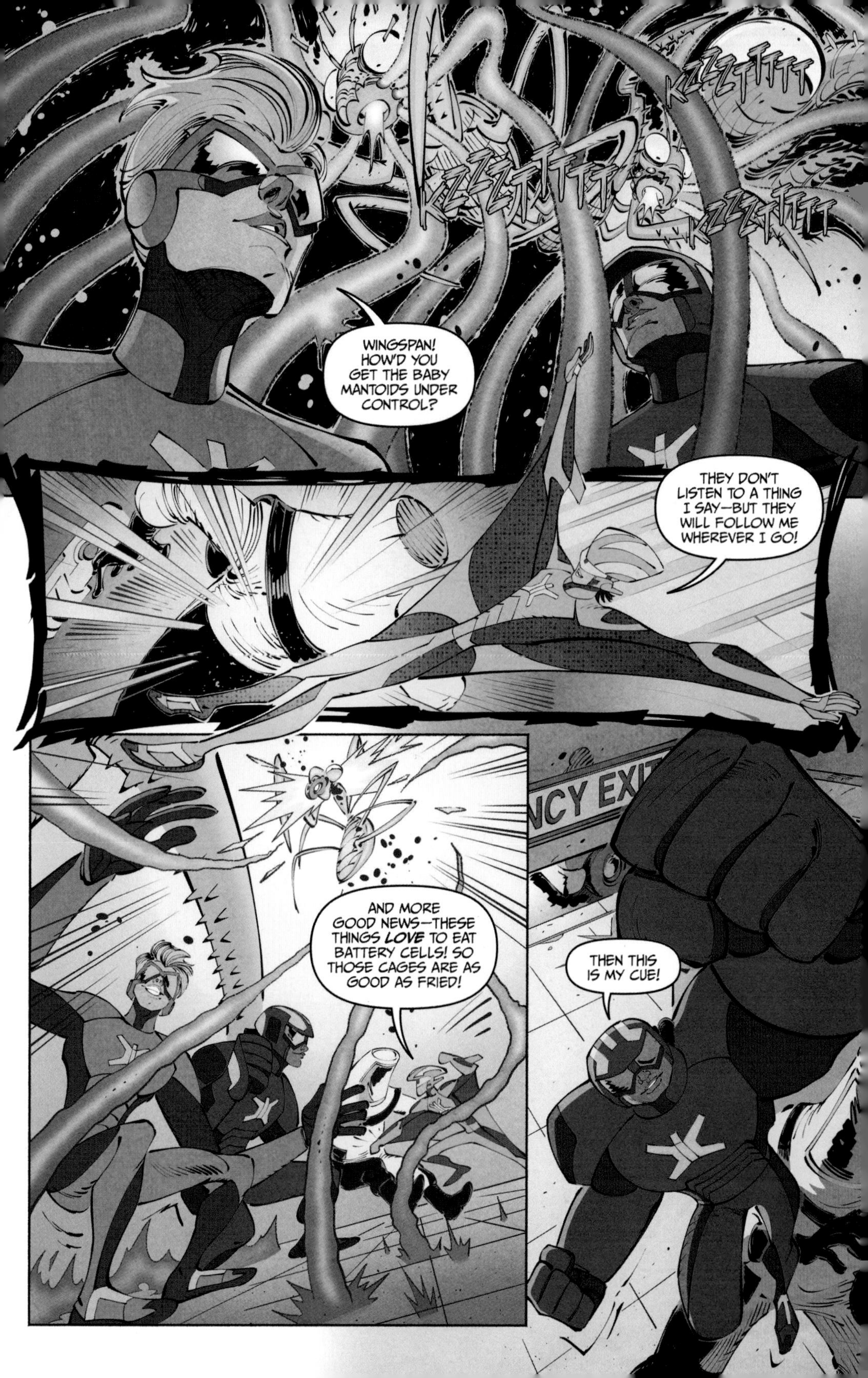
KZZZZTTTTT
KZZZZTTTTTTT
KZZZZTTTTTT
WINGSPAN! HOW'D YOU GET THE BABY MANTOIDS UNDER CONTROL?
THEY DON'T LISTEN TO A THING I SAY—BUT THEY WILL FOLLOW ME WHEREVER I GO!
AND MORE GOOD NEWS—THESE THINGS LOVE TO EAT BATTERY CELLS! SO THOSE CAGES ARE AS GOOD AS FRIED!
NCY EXIT
THEN THIS IS MY CUE!

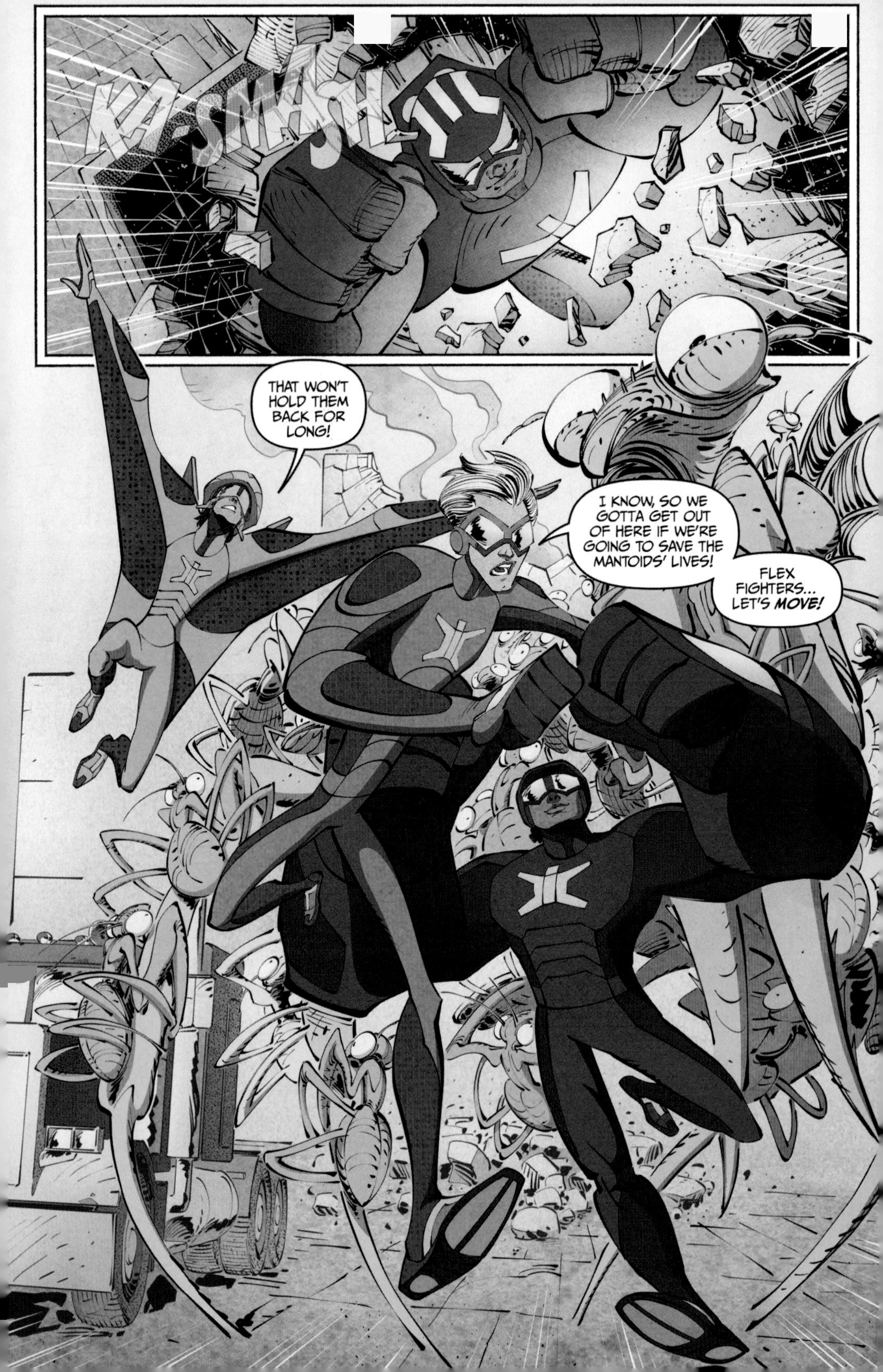
KA-SMASH!
THAT WON'T HOLD THEM BACK FOR LONG!
I KNOW, SO WE GOTTA GET OUT OF HERE IF WE'RE GOING TO SAVE THE MANTOIDS' LIVES!
FLEX FIGHTERS... LET'S *MOVE!*

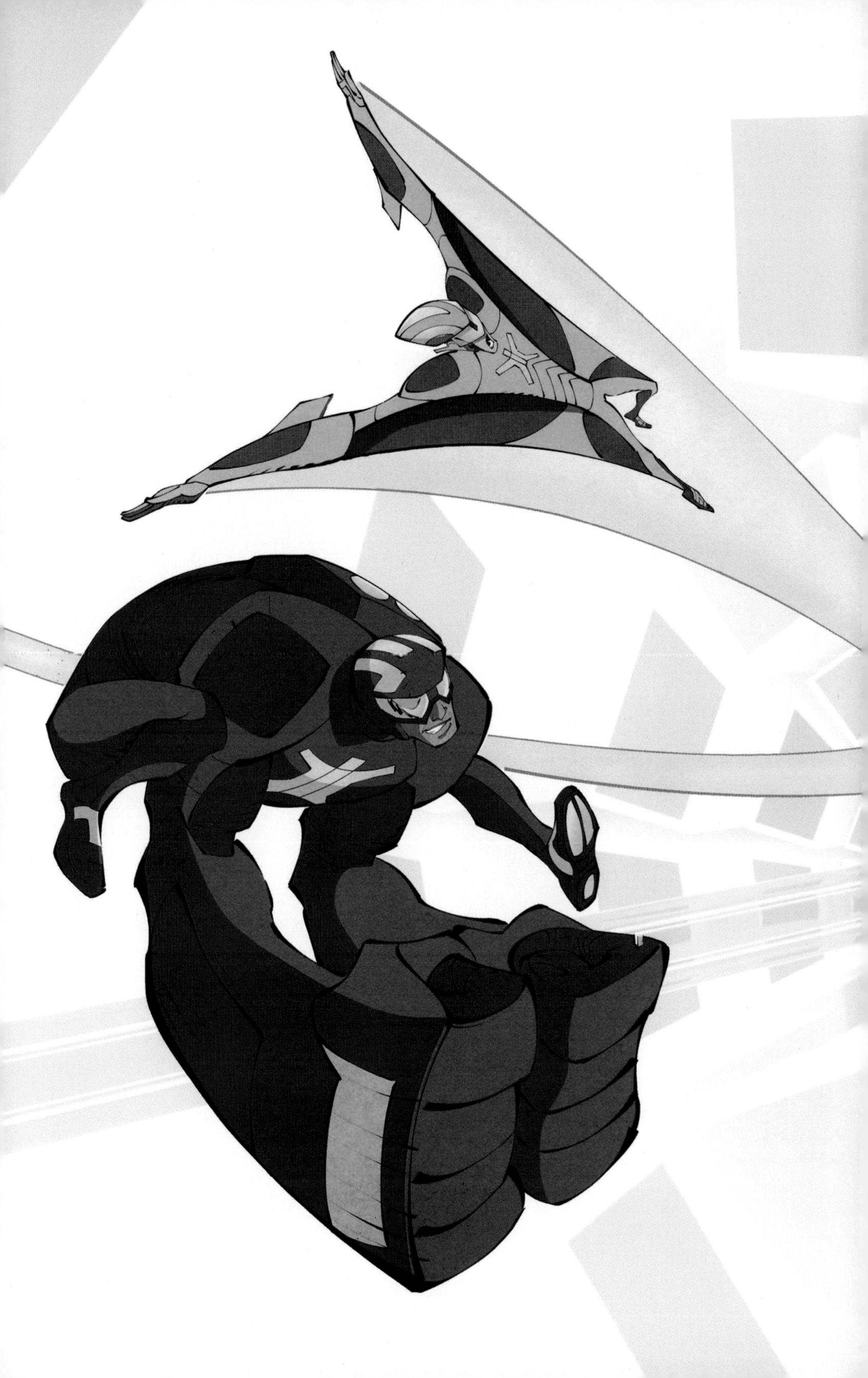

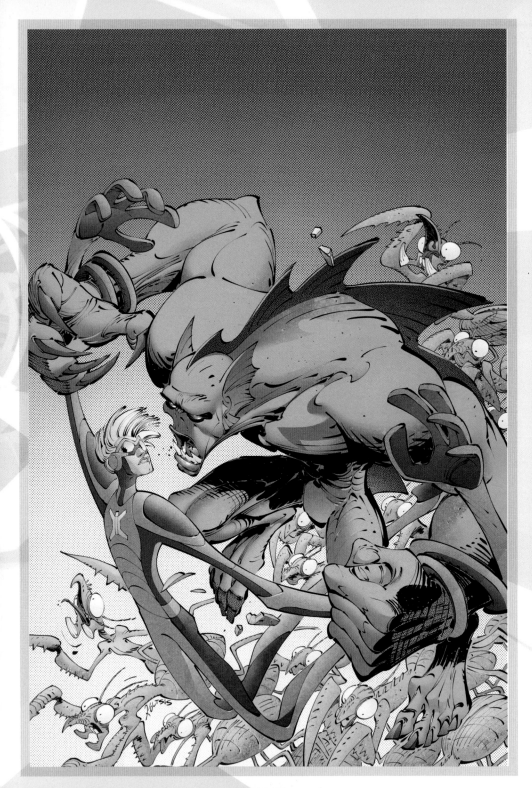

COVER ART
NIKOS KOUTSIS

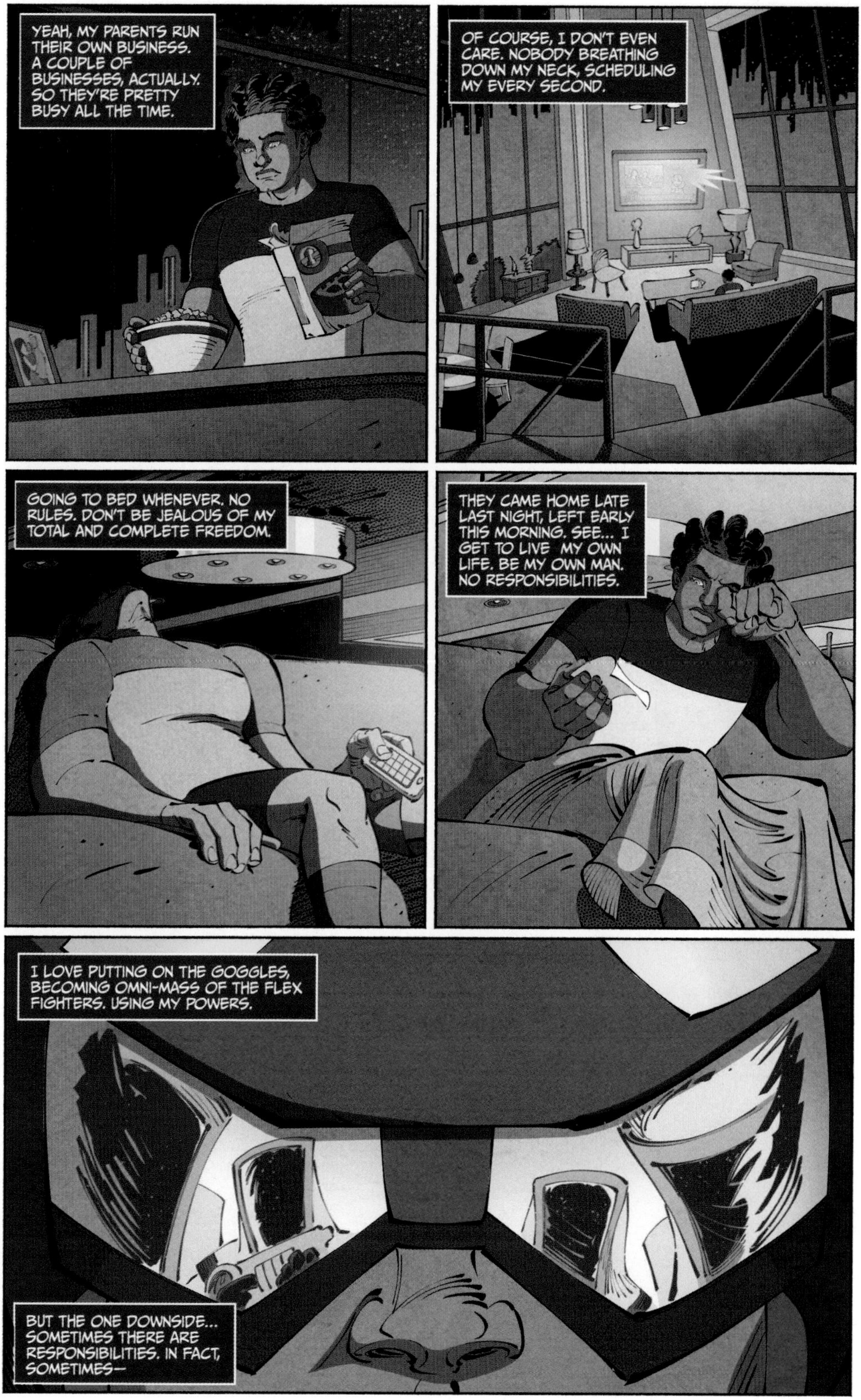
YEAH, MY PARENTS RUN THEIR OWN BUSINESS. A COUPLE OF BUSINESSES, ACTUALLY. SO THEY'RE PRETTY BUSY ALL THE TIME.
OF COURSE, I DON'T EVEN CARE. NOBODY BREATHING DOWN MY NECK, SCHEDULING MY EVERY SECOND.
GOING TO BED WHENEVER. NO RULES. DON'T BE JEALOUS OF MY TOTAL AND COMPLETE FREEDOM.
THEY CAME HOME LATE LAST NIGHT, LEFT EARLY THIS MORNING. SEE... I GET TO LIVE MY OWN LIFE. BE MY OWN MAN. NO RESPONSIBILITIES.
I LOVE PUTTING ON THE GOGGLES, BECOMING OMNI-MASS OF THE FLEX FIGHTERS. USING MY POWERS.
BUT THE ONE DOWNSIDE... SOMETIMES THERE ARE RESPONSIBILITIES. IN FACT, SOMETIMES—

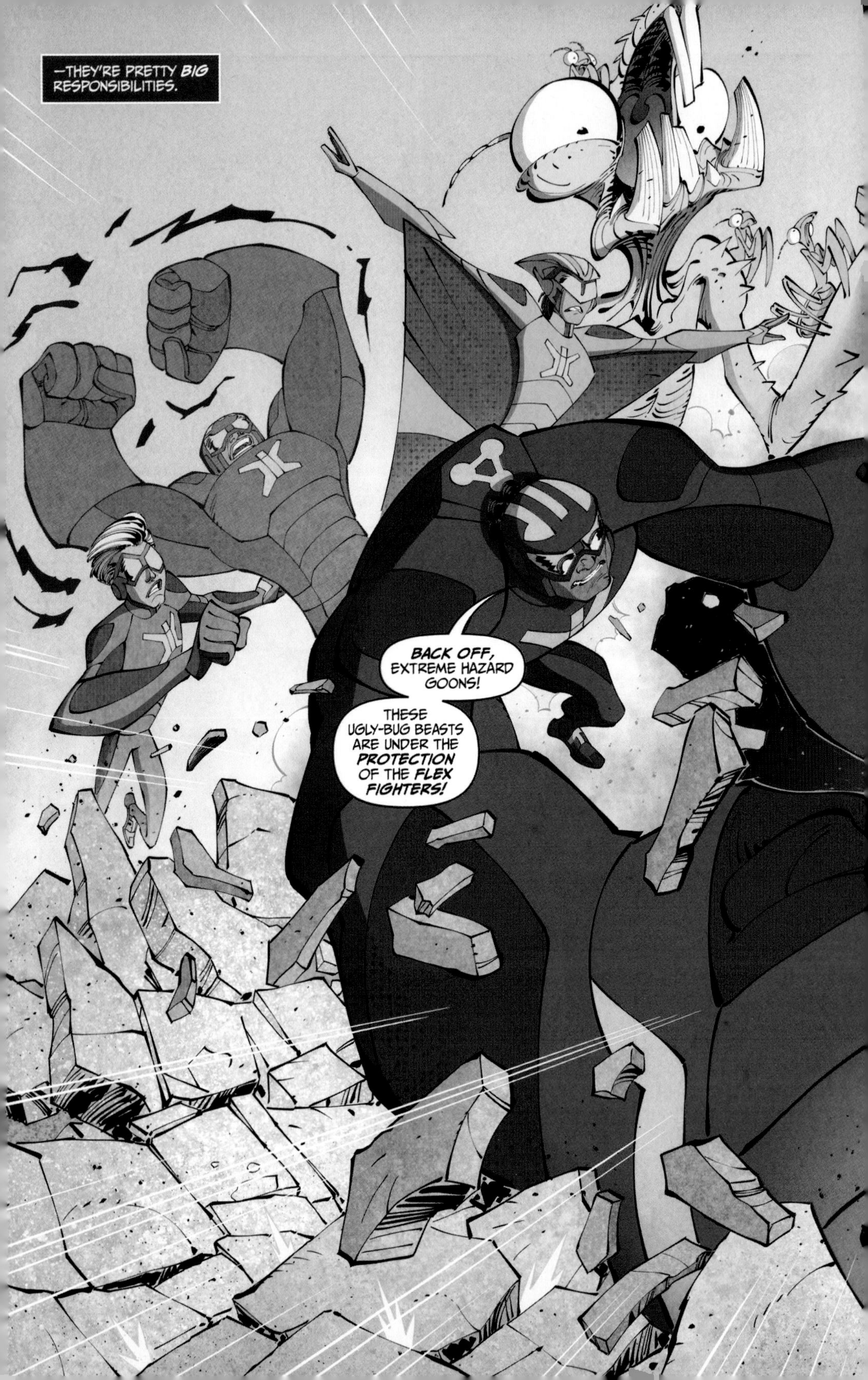
—THEY'RE PRETTY BIG RESPONSIBILITIES.
BACK OFF, EXTREME HAZARD GOONS!
THESE UGLY-BUG BEASTS ARE UNDER THE PROTECTION OF THE FLEX FIGHTERS!

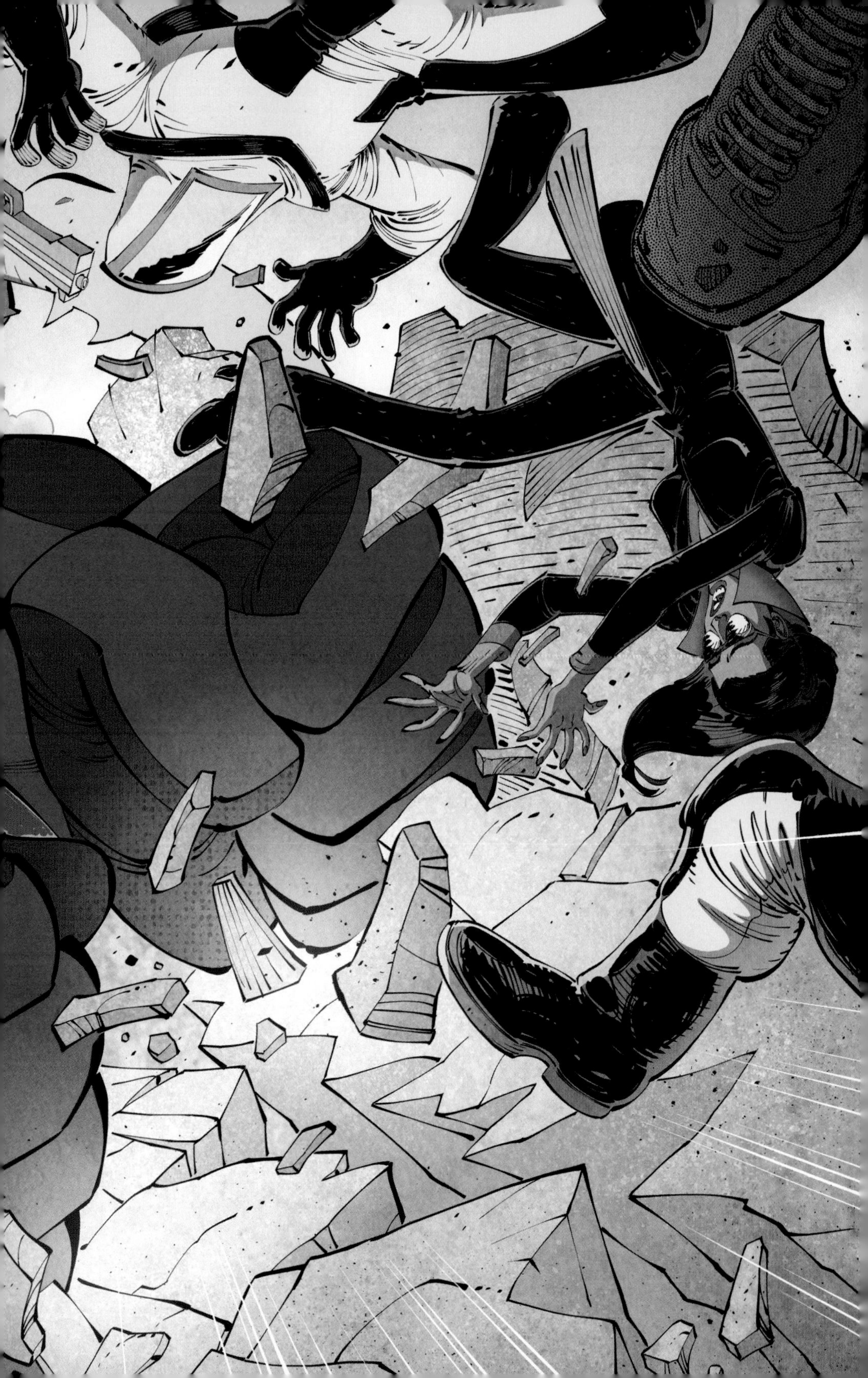

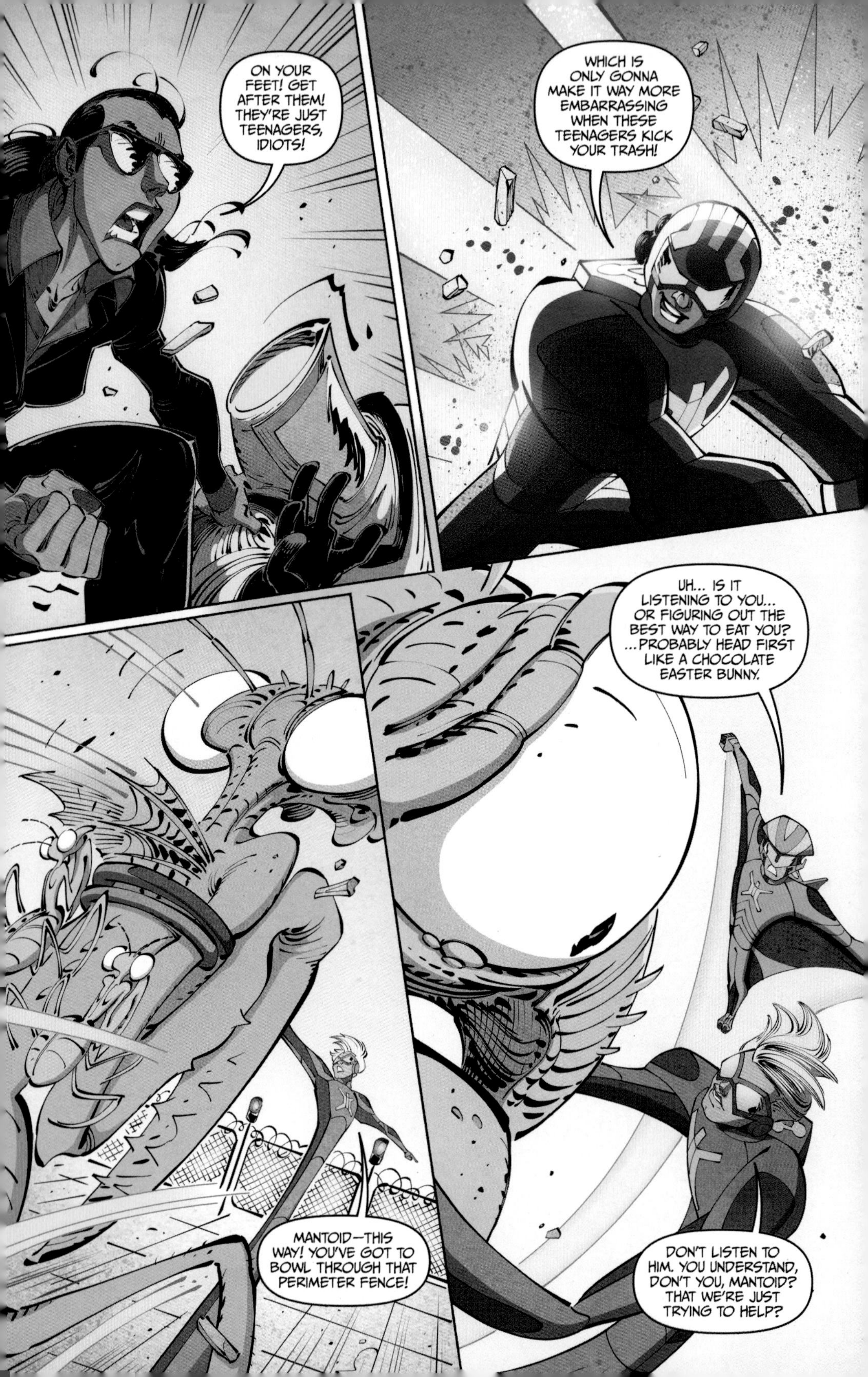
ON YOUR FEET! GET AFTER THEM! THEY'RE JUST TEENAGERS, IDIOTS!
WHICH IS ONLY GONNA MAKE IT WAY MORE EMBARRASSING WHEN THESE TEENAGERS KICK YOUR TRASH!
UH... IS IT LISTENING TO YOU... OR FIGURING OUT THE BEST WAY TO EAT YOU? ...PROBABLY HEAD FIRST LIKE A CHOCOLATE EASTER BUNNY.
MANTOID—THIS WAY! YOU'VE GOT TO BOWL THROUGH THAT PERIMETER FENCE!
DON'T LISTEN TO HIM. YOU UNDERSTAND, DON'T YOU, MANTOID? THAT WE'RE JUST TRYING TO HELP?

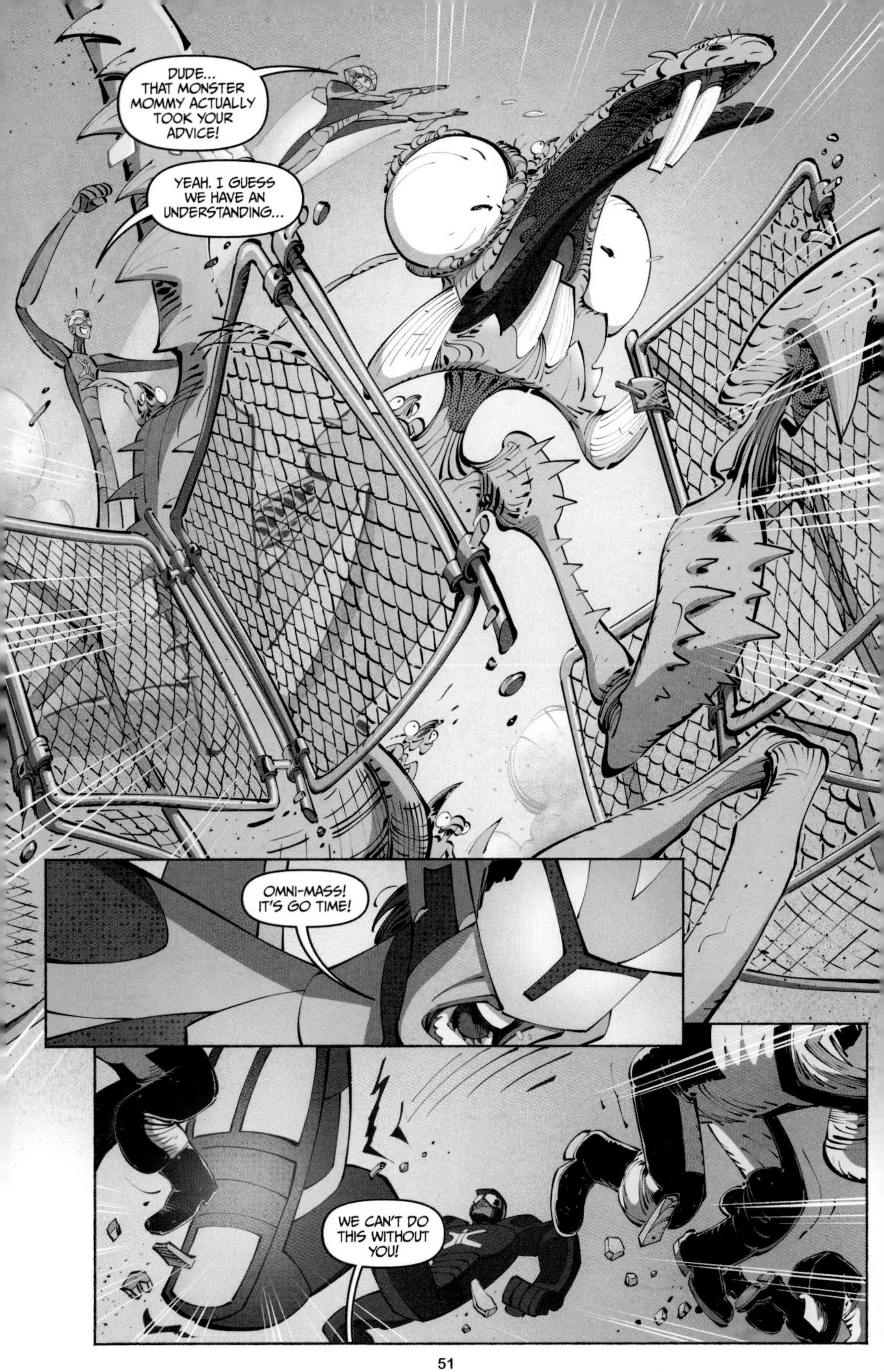
DUDE... THAT MONSTER MOMMY ACTUALLY TOOK YOUR ADVICE!
YEAH. I GUESS WE HAVE AN UNDERSTANDING...
OMNI-MASS! IT'S GO TIME!
WE CAN'T DO THIS WITHOUT YOU!

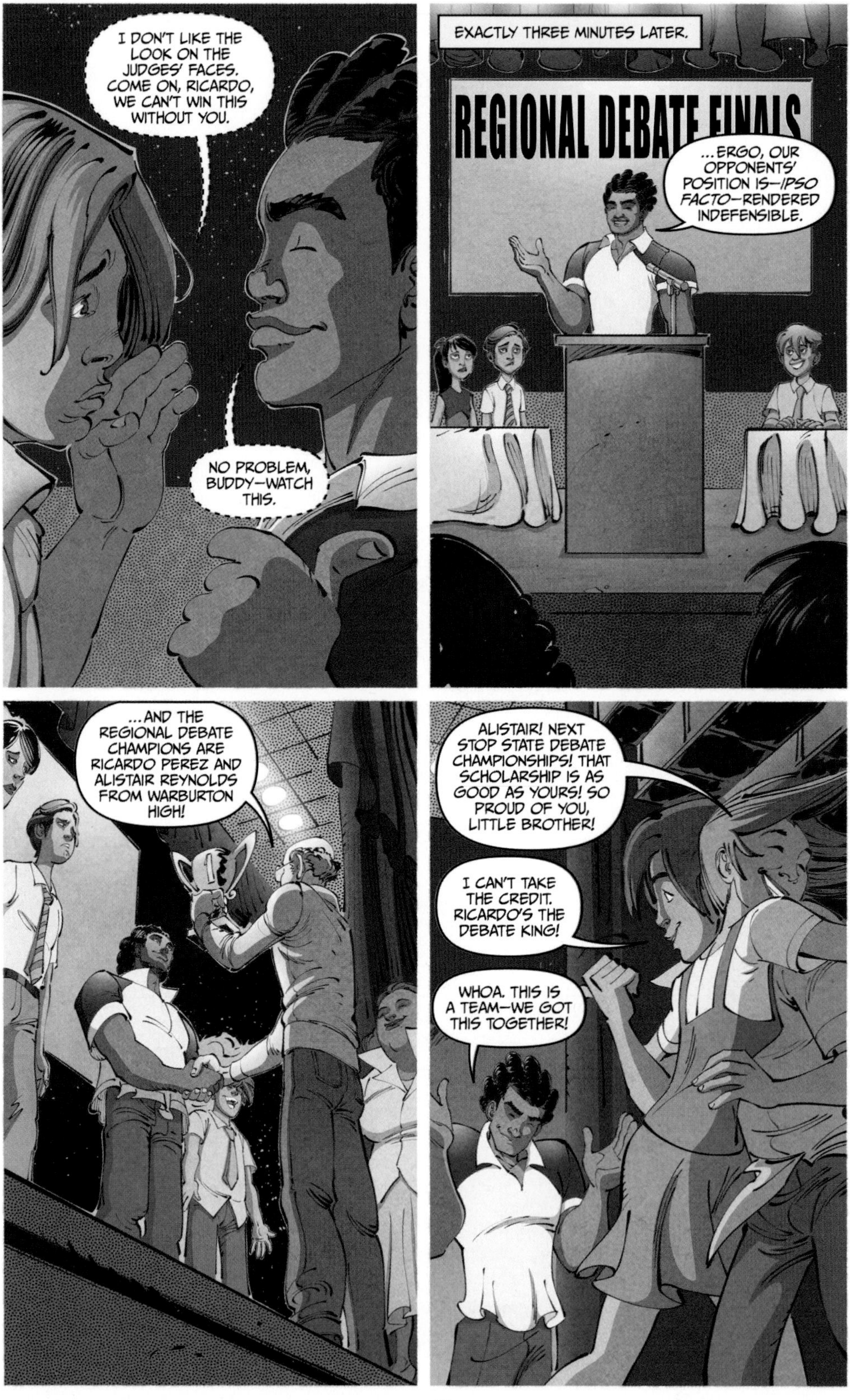
I DON'T LIKE THE LOOK ON THE JUDGES' FACES. COME ON, RICARDO, WE CAN'T WIN THIS WITHOUT YOU.
NO PROBLEM, BUDDY—WATCH THIS.
EXACTLY THREE MINUTES LATER.
REGIONAL DEBATE FINALS
...ERGO, OUR OPPONENTS' POSITION IS—*IPSO FACTO*—RENDERED INDEFENSIBLE.
...AND THE REGIONAL DEBATE CHAMPIONS ARE RICARDO PEREZ AND ALISTAIR REYNOLDS FROM WARBURTON HIGH!
ALISTAIR! NEXT STOP STATE DEBATE CHAMPIONSHIPS! THAT SCHOLARSHIP IS AS GOOD AS YOURS! SO PROUD OF YOU, LITTLE BROTHER!
I CAN'T TAKE THE CREDIT. RICARDO'S THE DEBATE KING!
WHOA. THIS IS A TEAM—WE GOT THIS TOGETHER!

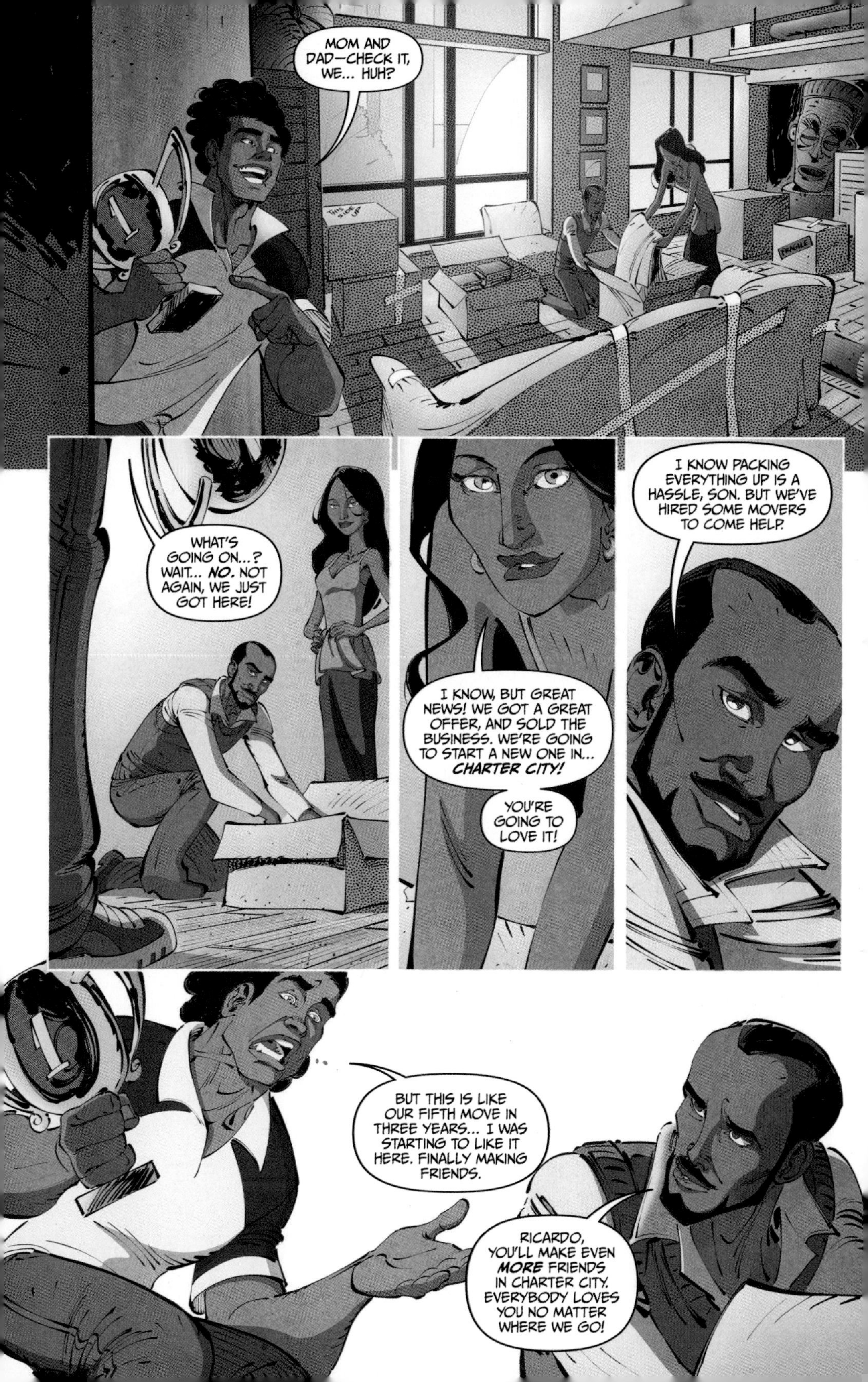
MOM AND DAD—CHECK IT, WE... HUH?
THIS SIDE UP
FRAGILE
WHAT'S GOING ON...? WAIT... NO. NOT AGAIN, WE JUST GOT HERE!
I KNOW, BUT GREAT NEWS! WE GOT A GREAT OFFER, AND SOLD THE BUSINESS. WE'RE GOING TO START A NEW ONE IN... CHARTER CITY!
YOU'RE GOING TO LOVE IT!
I KNOW PACKING EVERYTHING UP IS A HASSLE, SON. BUT WE'VE HIRED SOME MOVERS TO COME HELP.
BUT THIS IS LIKE OUR FIFTH MOVE IN THREE YEARS... I WAS STARTING TO LIKE IT HERE. FINALLY MAKING FRIENDS.
RICARDO, YOU'LL MAKE EVEN MORE FRIENDS IN CHARTER CITY. EVERYBODY LOVES YOU NO MATTER WHERE WE GO!

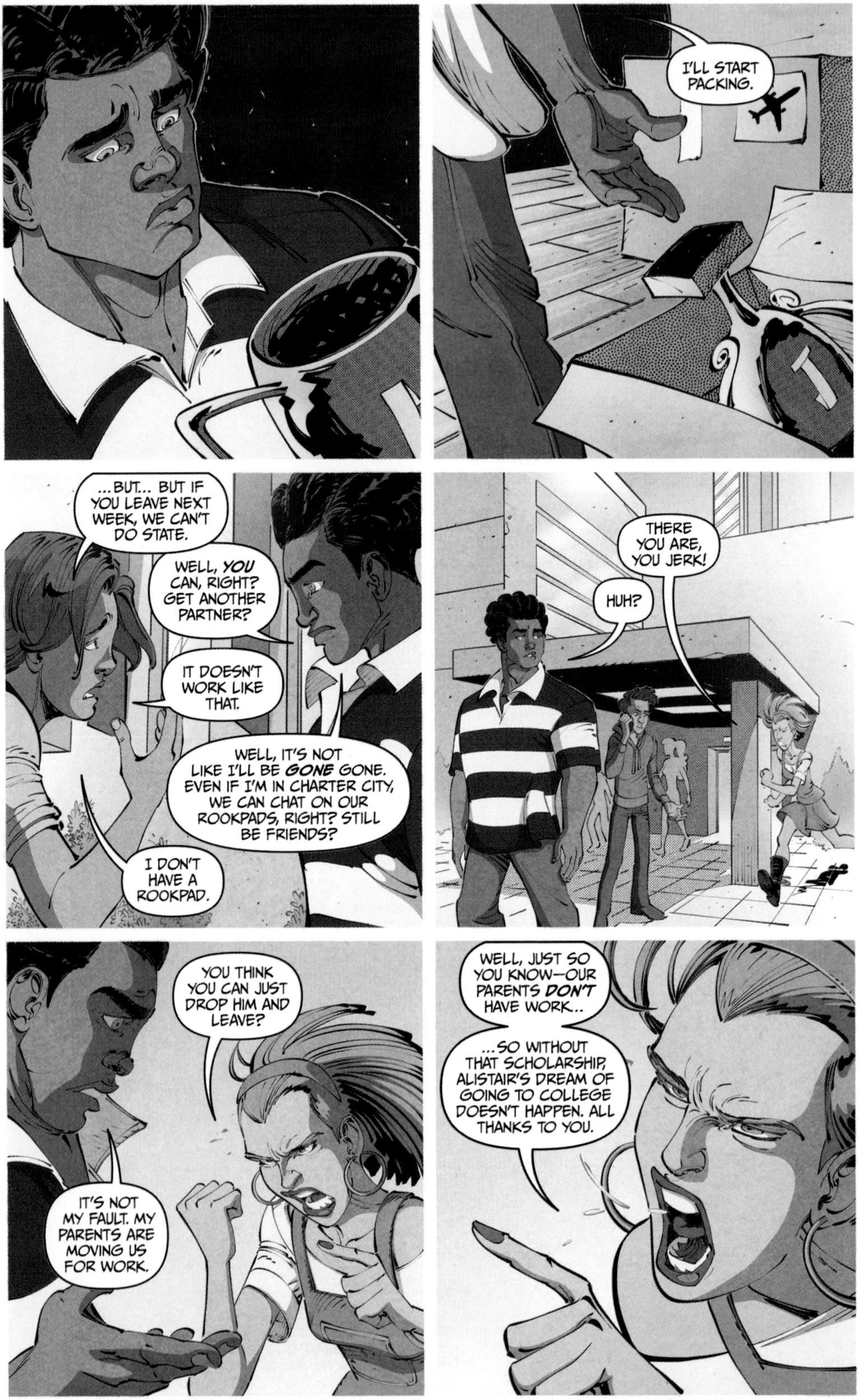
I'LL START PACKING.
...BUT... BUT IF YOU LEAVE NEXT WEEK, WE CAN'T DO STATE.
WELL, *YOU* CAN, RIGHT? GET ANOTHER PARTNER?
IT DOESN'T WORK LIKE THAT.
WELL, IT'S NOT LIKE I'LL BE ***GONE*** GONE. EVEN IF I'M IN CHARTER CITY, WE CAN CHAT ON OUR ROOKPADS, RIGHT? STILL BE FRIENDS?
I DON'T HAVE A ROOKPAD.
THERE YOU ARE, YOU JERK!
HUH?
YOU THINK YOU CAN JUST DROP HIM AND LEAVE?
IT'S NOT MY FAULT. MY PARENTS ARE MOVING US FOR WORK.
WELL, JUST SO YOU KNOW—OUR PARENTS ***DON'T*** HAVE WORK...
...SO WITHOUT THAT SCHOLARSHIP, ALISTAIR'S DREAM OF GOING TO COLLEGE DOESN'T HAPPEN. ALL THANKS TO YOU.

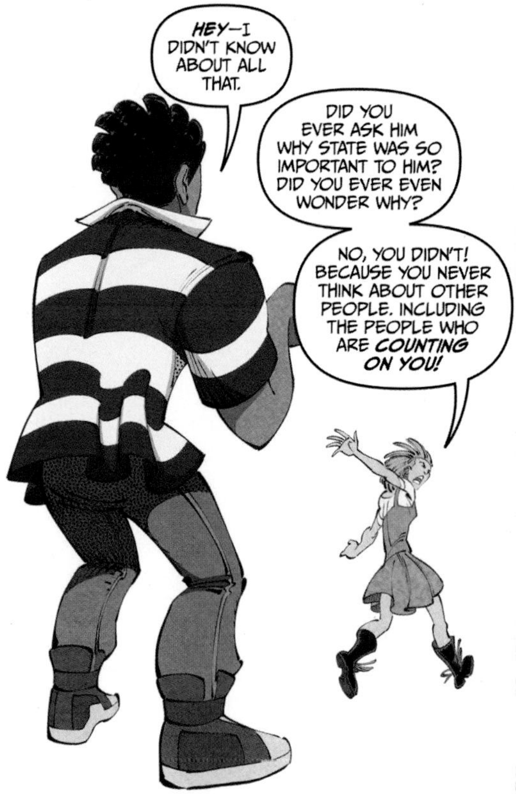
HEY—I DIDN'T KNOW ABOUT ALL THAT.
DID YOU EVER ASK HIM WHY STATE WAS SO IMPORTANT TO HIM? DID YOU EVER EVEN WONDER WHY?
NO, YOU DIDN'T! BECAUSE YOU NEVER THINK ABOUT OTHER PEOPLE. INCLUDING THE PEOPLE WHO ARE COUNTING ON YOU!

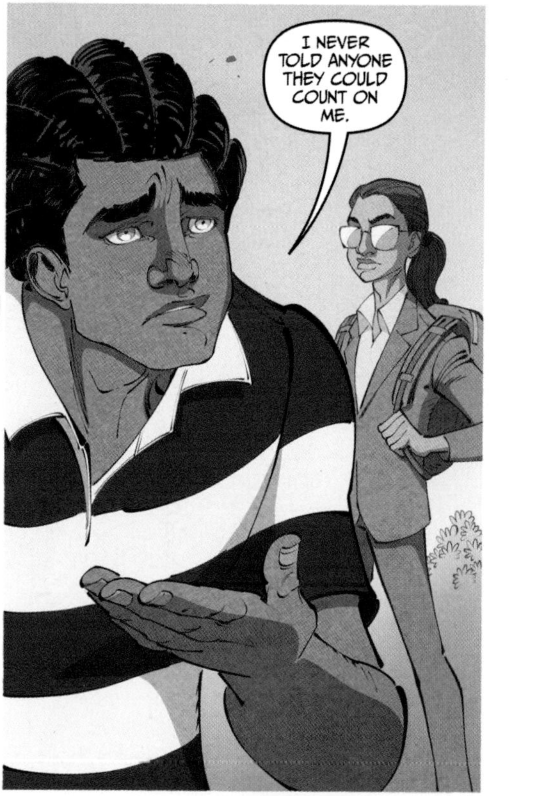
I NEVER TOLD ANYONE THEY COULD COUNT ON ME.

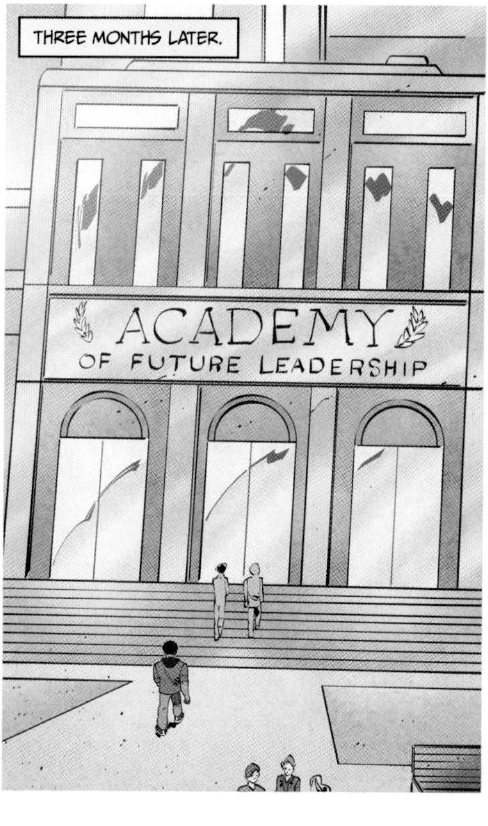
THREE MONTHS LATER.
ACADEMY OF FUTURE LEADERSHIP

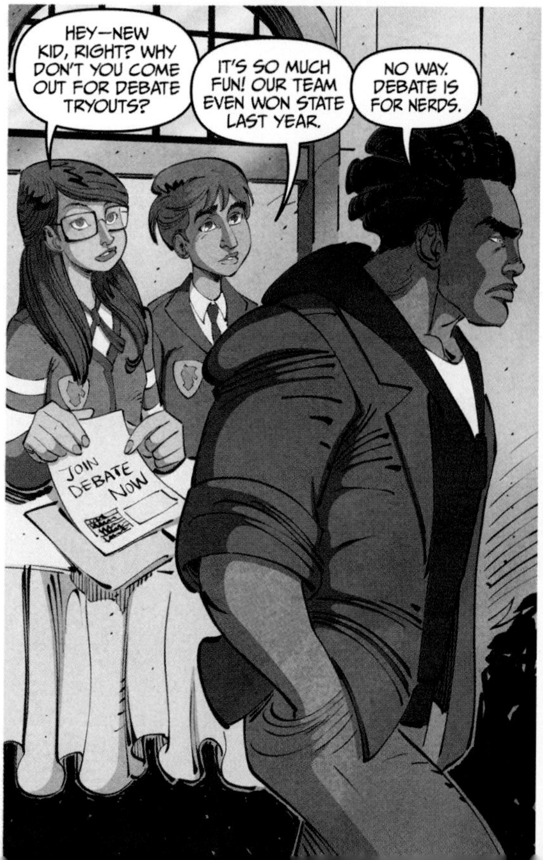
HEY—NEW KID, RIGHT? WHY DON'T YOU COME OUT FOR DEBATE TRYOUTS?
IT'S SO MUCH FUN! OUR TEAM EVEN WON STATE LAST YEAR.
NO WAY. DEBATE IS FOR NERDS.
JOIN DEBATE NOW

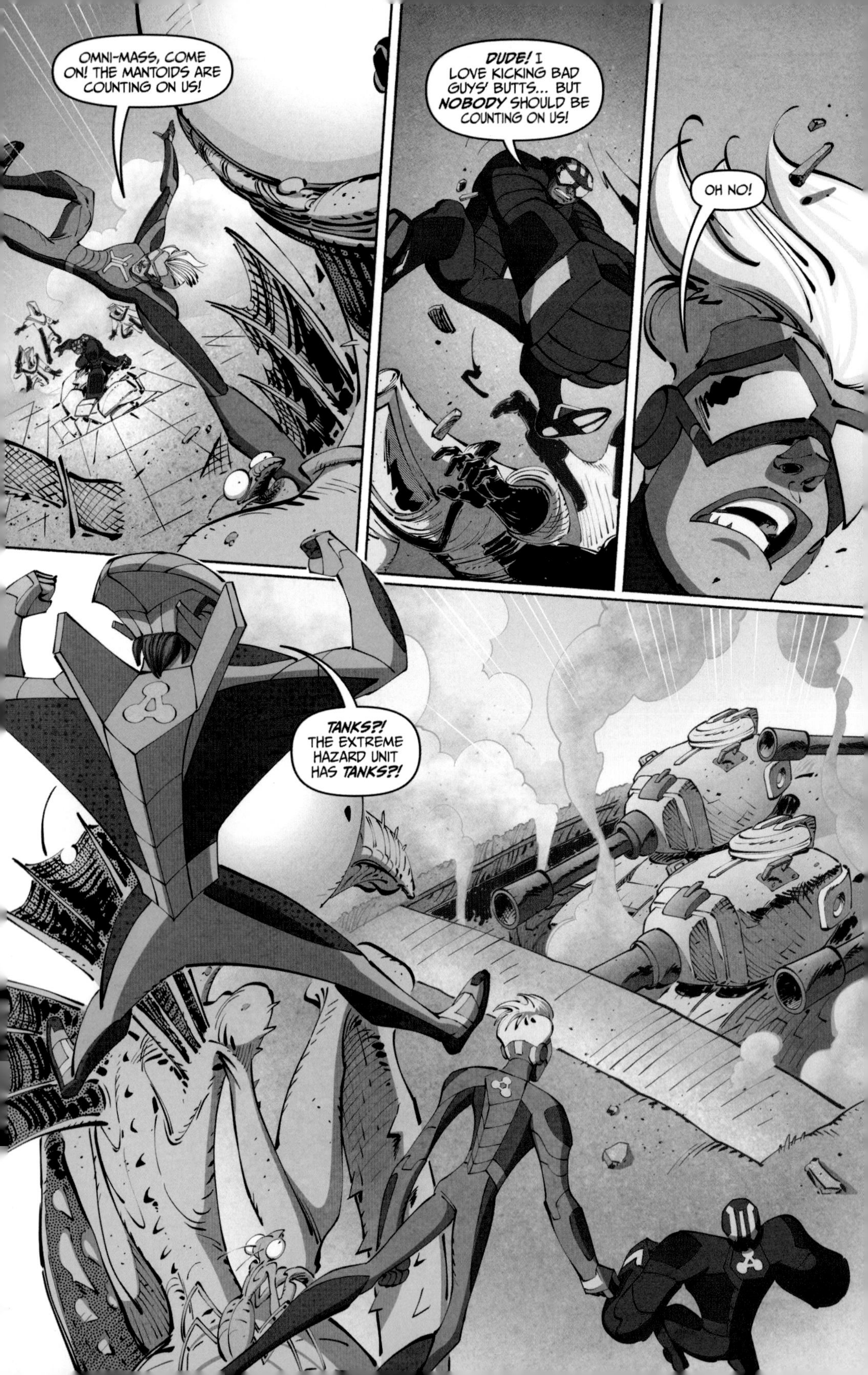
OMNI-MASS, COME ON! THE MANTOIDS ARE COUNTING ON US!
DUDE! I LOVE KICKING BAD GUYS' BUTTS... BUT NOBODY SHOULD BE COUNTING ON US!
OH NO!
TANKS?! THE EXTREME HAZARD UNIT HAS TANKS?!

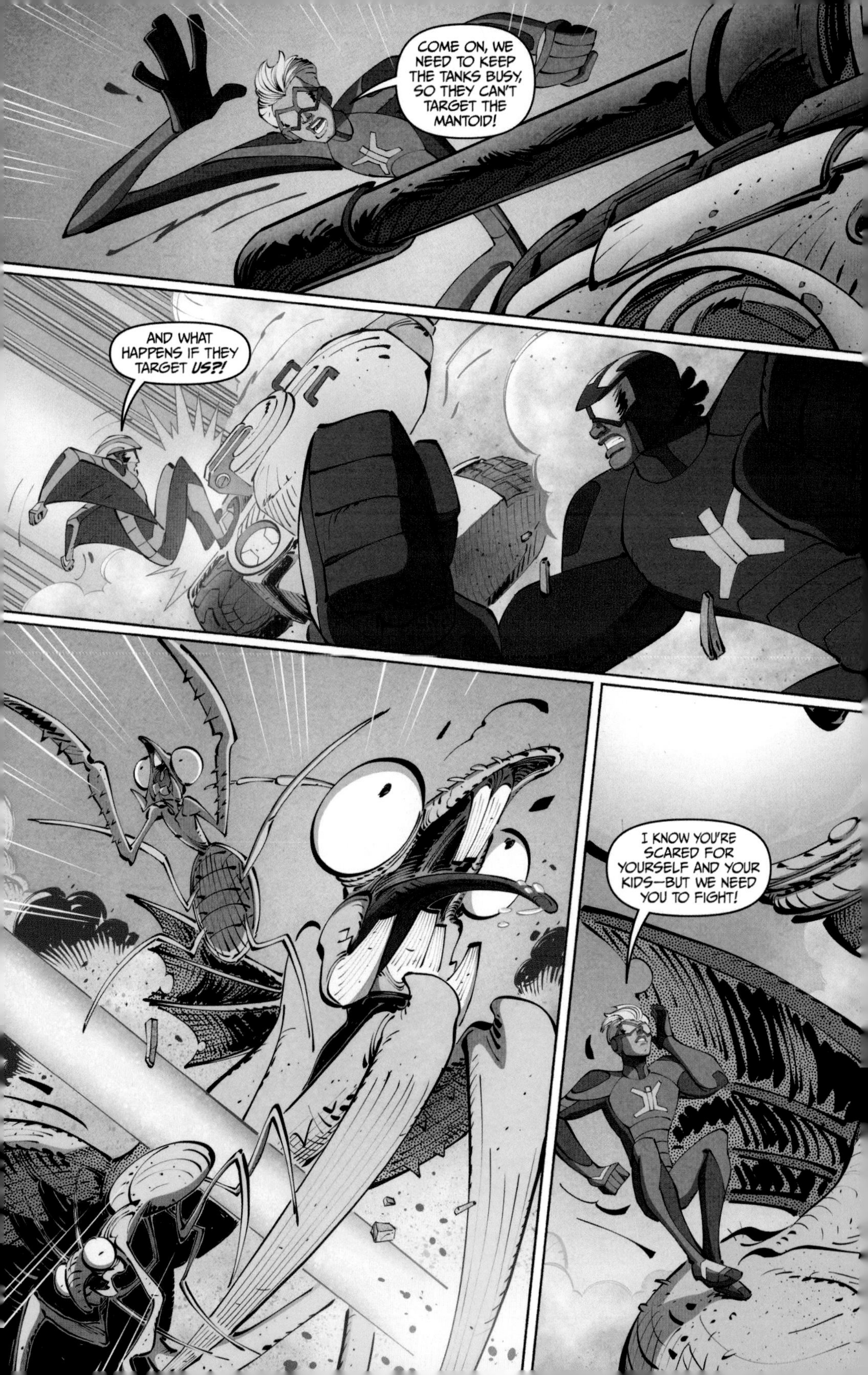
COME ON, WE NEED TO KEEP THE TANKS BUSY, SO THEY CAN'T TARGET THE MANTOID!
AND WHAT HAPPENS IF THEY TARGET *US?!*
I KNOW YOU'RE SCARED FOR YOURSELF AND YOUR KIDS—BUT WE NEED YOU TO FIGHT!

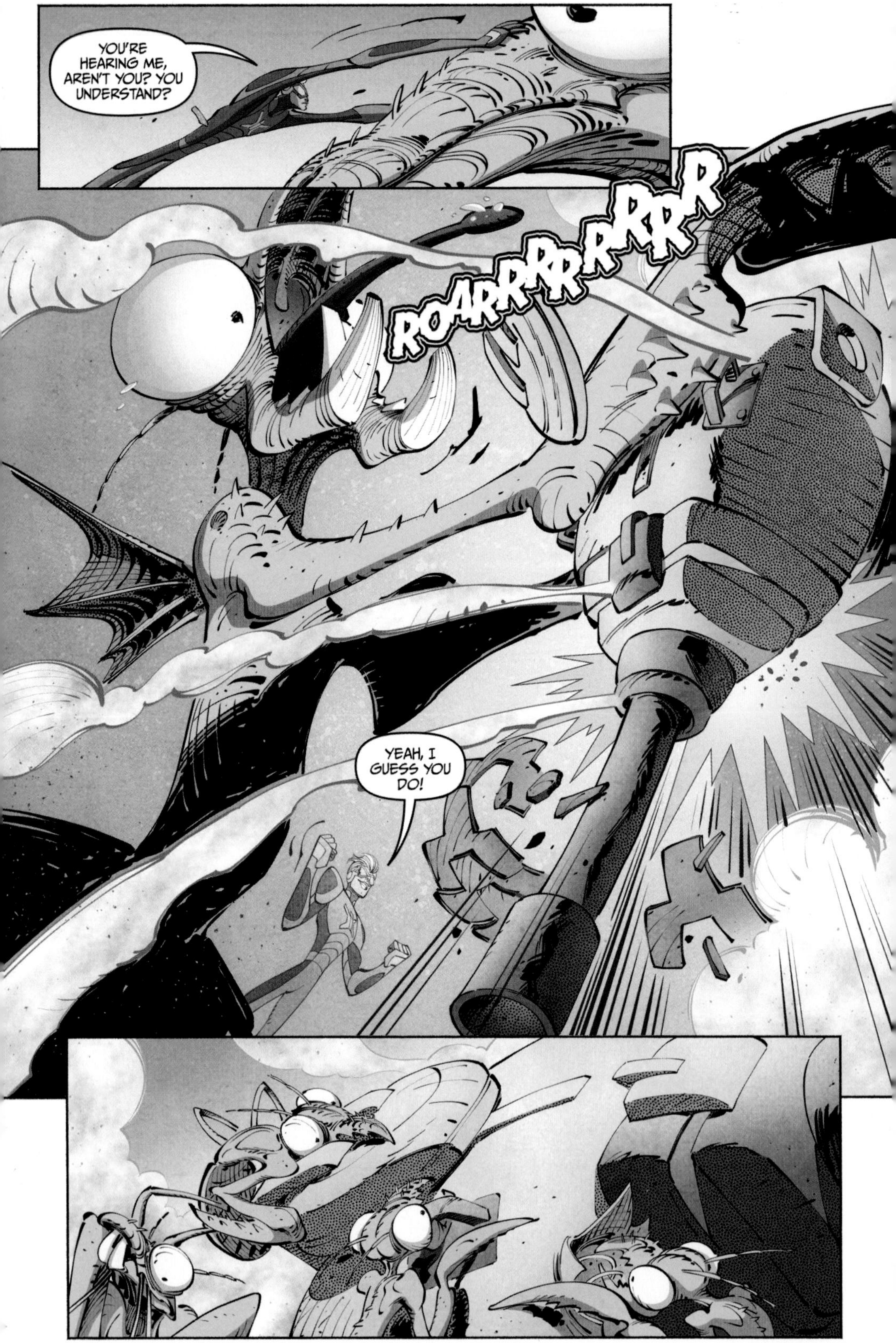
YOU'RE HEARING ME, AREN'T YOU? YOU UNDERSTAND?
ROARRRRRRRRR
YEAH, I GUESS YOU DO!

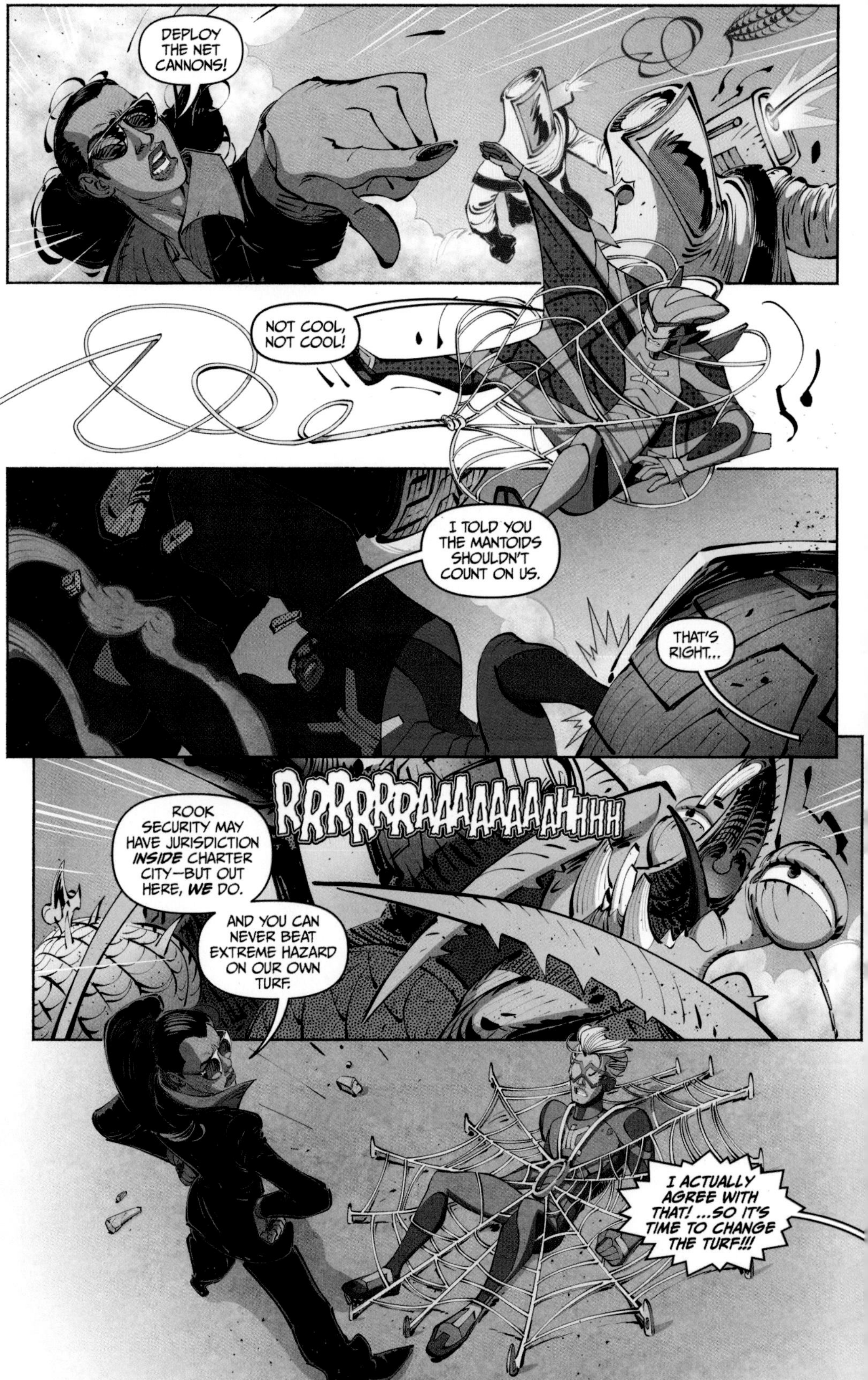
DEPLOY THE NET CANNONS!
NOT COOL, NOT COOL!
I TOLD YOU THE MANTOIDS SHOULDN'T COUNT ON US.
THAT'S RIGHT...
RRRRRRAAAAAAAAHHHH
ROOK SECURITY MAY HAVE JURISDICTION *INSIDE* CHARTER CITY—BUT OUT HERE, *WE* DO.
AND YOU CAN NEVER BEAT EXTREME HAZARD ON OUR OWN TURF.
I ACTUALLY AGREE WITH THAT! ...SO IT'S TIME TO CHANGE THE TURF!!!

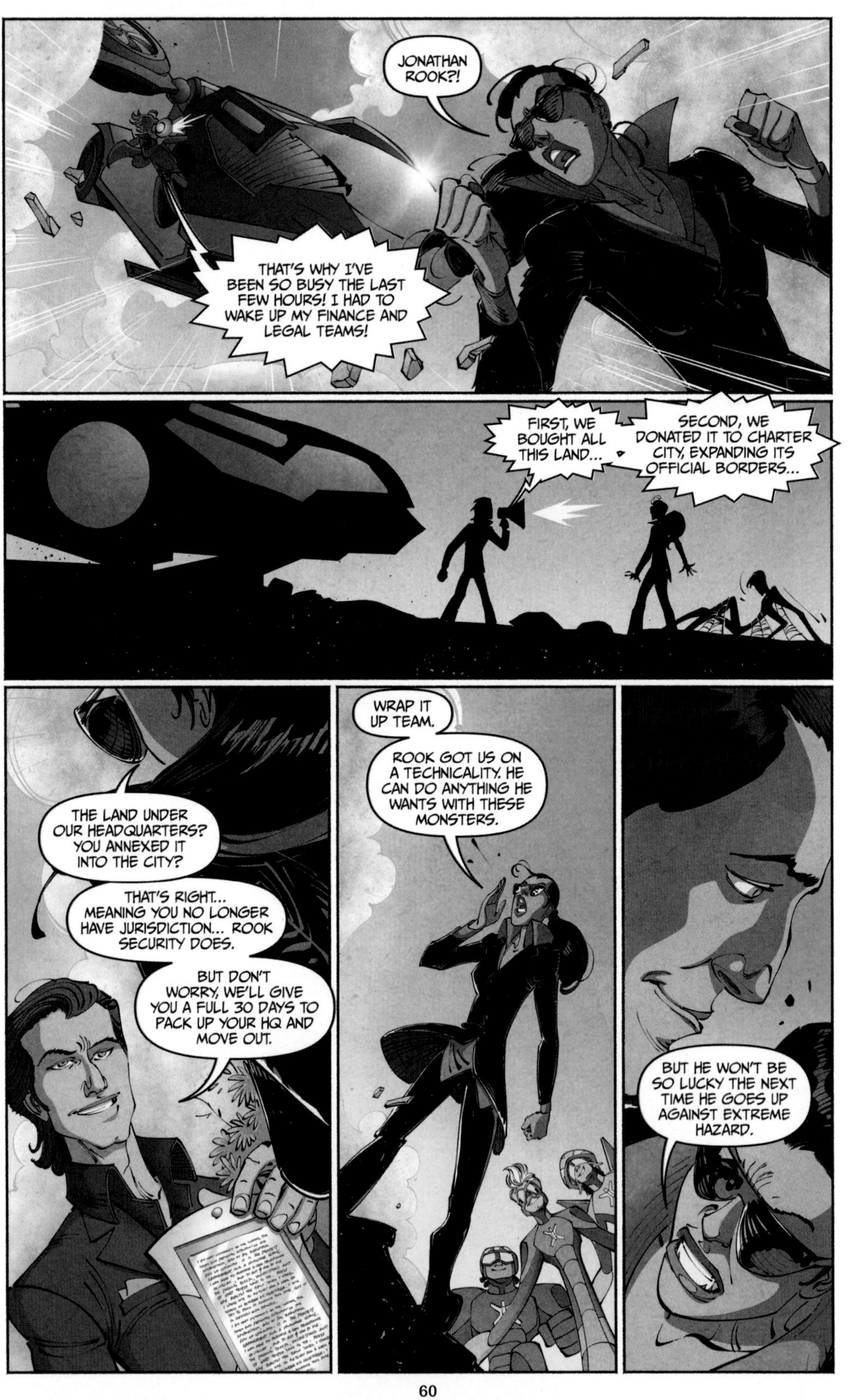
JONATHAN ROOK?!
THAT'S WHY I'VE BEEN SO BUSY THE LAST FEW HOURS! I HAD TO WAKE UP MY FINANCE AND LEGAL TEAMS!
FIRST, WE BOUGHT ALL THIS LAND...
SECOND, WE DONATED IT TO CHARTER CITY, EXPANDING ITS OFFICIAL BORDERS...
THE LAND UNDER OUR HEADQUARTERS? YOU ANNEXED IT INTO THE CITY?
THAT'S RIGHT... MEANING YOU NO LONGER HAVE JURISDICTION... ROOK SECURITY DOES.
BUT DON'T WORRY, WE'LL GIVE YOU A FULL 30 DAYS TO PACK UP YOUR HQ AND MOVE OUT.
WRAP IT UP TEAM.
ROOK GOT US ON A TECHNICALITY. HE CAN DO ANYTHING HE WANTS WITH THESE MONSTERS.
BUT HE WON'T BE SO LUCKY THE NEXT TIME HE GOES UP AGAINST EXTREME HAZARD.

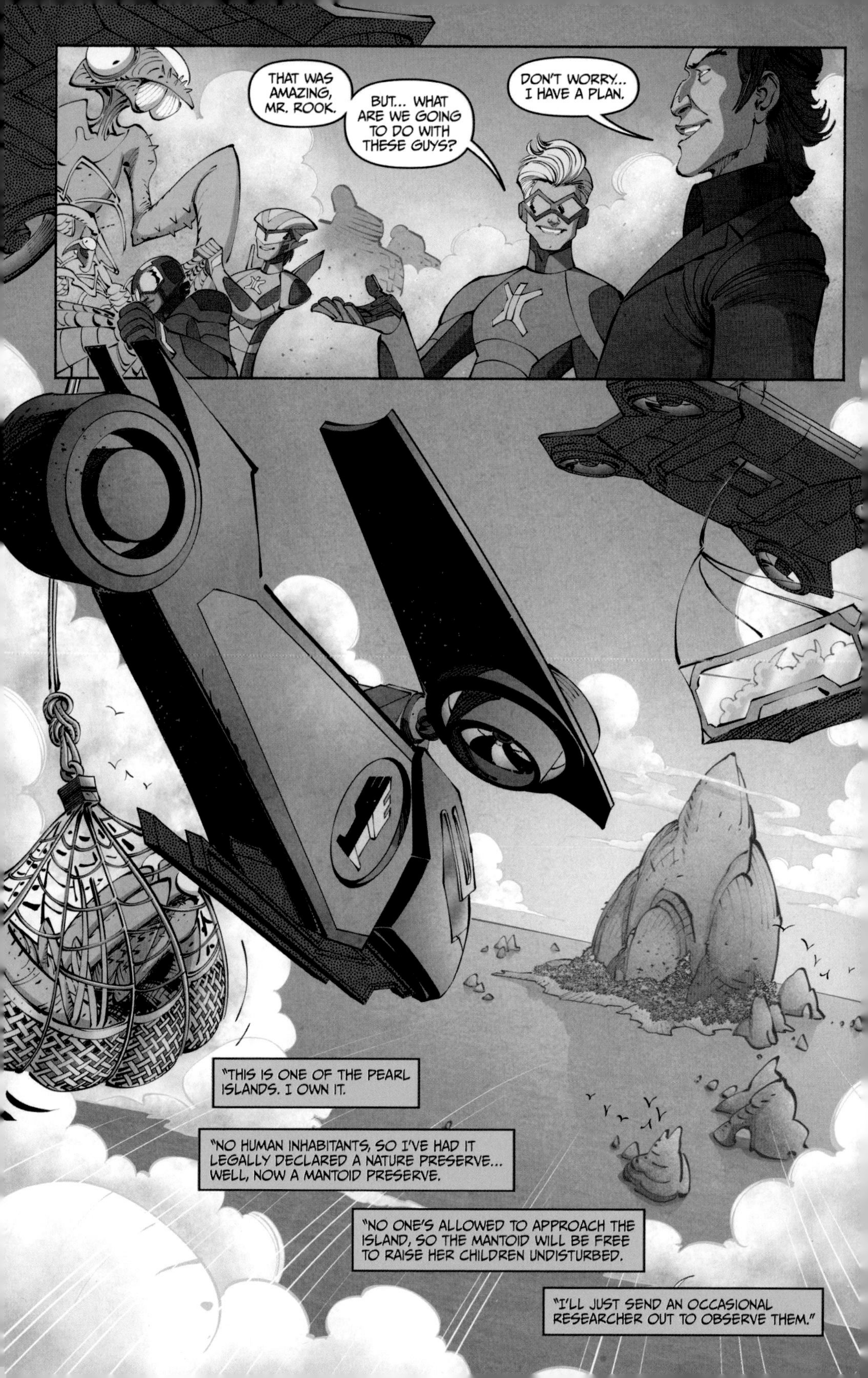
THAT WAS AMAZING, MR. ROOK.
BUT... WHAT ARE WE GOING TO DO WITH THESE GUYS?
DON'T WORRY... I HAVE A PLAN.
"THIS IS ONE OF THE PEARL ISLANDS. I OWN IT.
"NO HUMAN INHABITANTS, SO I'VE HAD IT LEGALLY DECLARED A NATURE PRESERVE... WELL, NOW A MANTOID PRESERVE.
"NO ONE'S ALLOWED TO APPROACH THE ISLAND, SO THE MANTOID WILL BE FREE TO RAISE HER CHILDREN UNDISTURBED.
"I'LL JUST SEND AN OCCASIONAL RESEARCHER OUT TO OBSERVE THEM."

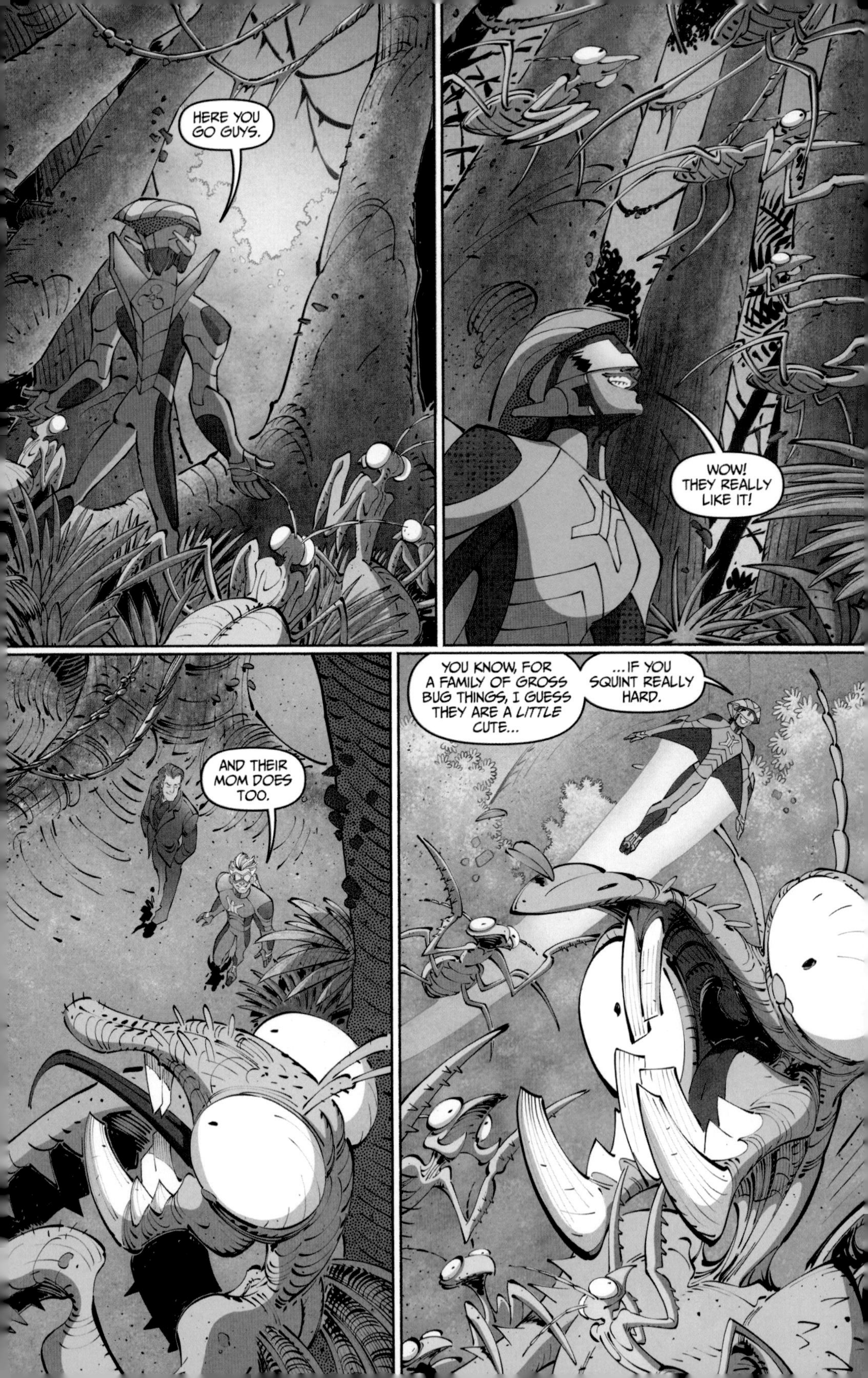
HERE YOU GO GUYS.
WOW! THEY REALLY LIKE IT!
AND THEIR MOM DOES TOO.
YOU KNOW, FOR A FAMILY OF GROSS BUG THINGS, I GUESS THEY ARE A *LITTLE* CUTE...
...IF YOU SQUINT REALLY HARD.

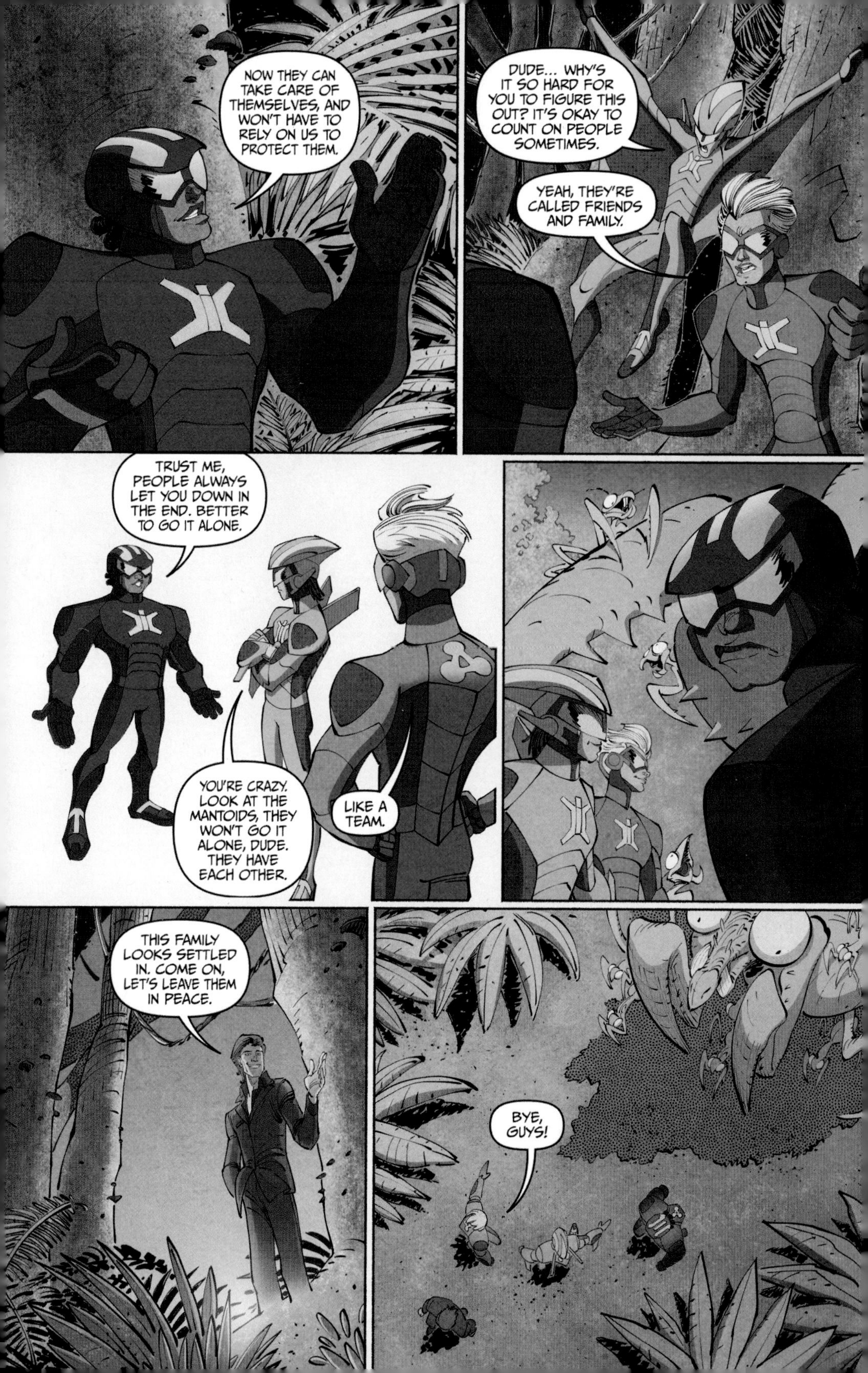
NOW THEY CAN TAKE CARE OF THEMSELVES, AND WON'T HAVE TO RELY ON US TO PROTECT THEM.
DUDE... WHY'S IT SO HARD FOR YOU TO FIGURE THIS OUT? IT'S OKAY TO COUNT ON PEOPLE SOMETIMES.
YEAH, THEY'RE CALLED FRIENDS AND FAMILY.
TRUST ME, PEOPLE ALWAYS LET YOU DOWN IN THE END. BETTER TO GO IT ALONE.
YOU'RE CRAZY. LOOK AT THE MANTOIDS, THEY WON'T GO IT ALONE, DUDE. THEY HAVE EACH OTHER.
LIKE A TEAM.
THIS FAMILY LOOKS SETTLED IN. COME ON, LET'S LEAVE THEM IN PEACE.
BYE, GUYS!

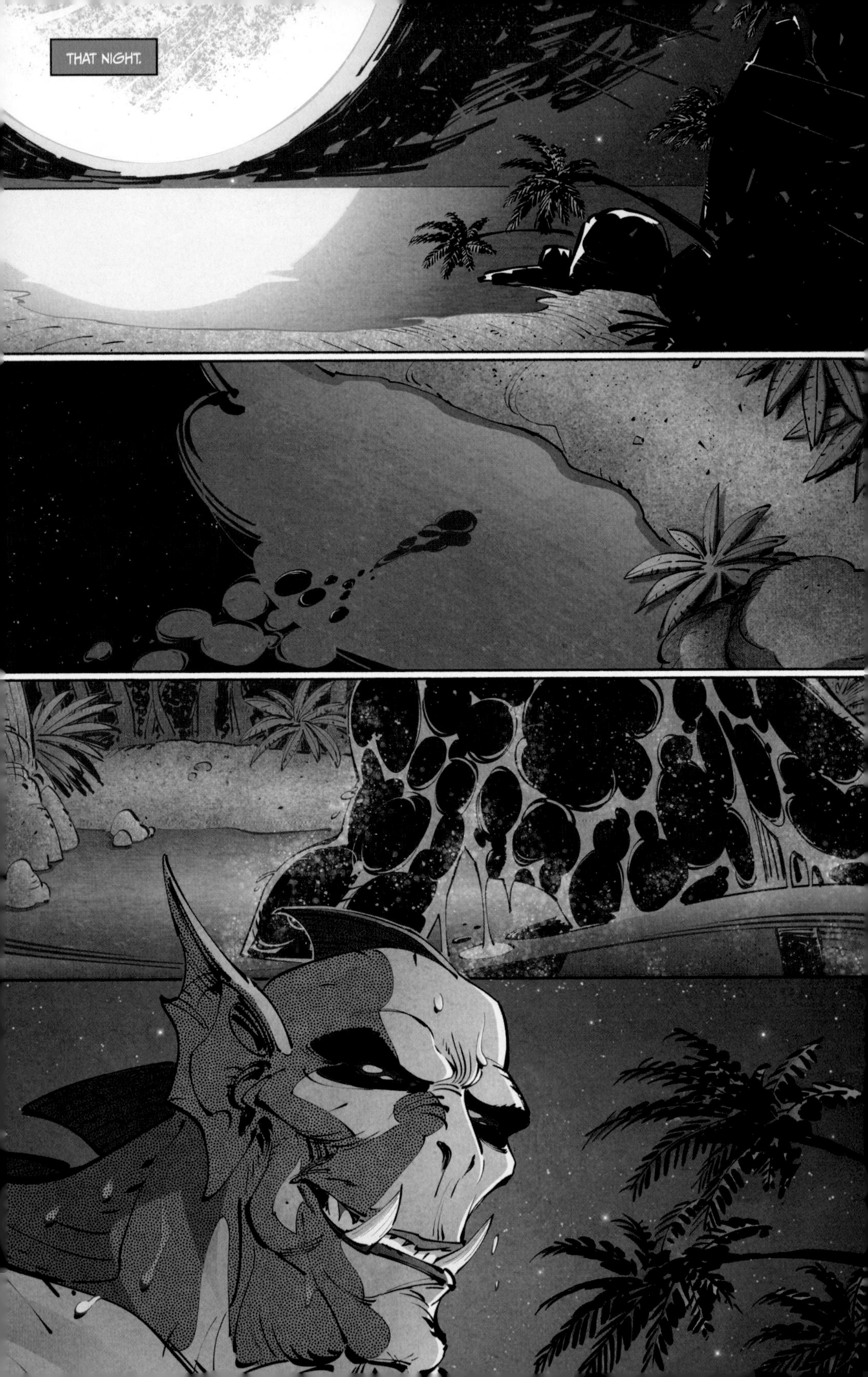
THAT NIGHT.

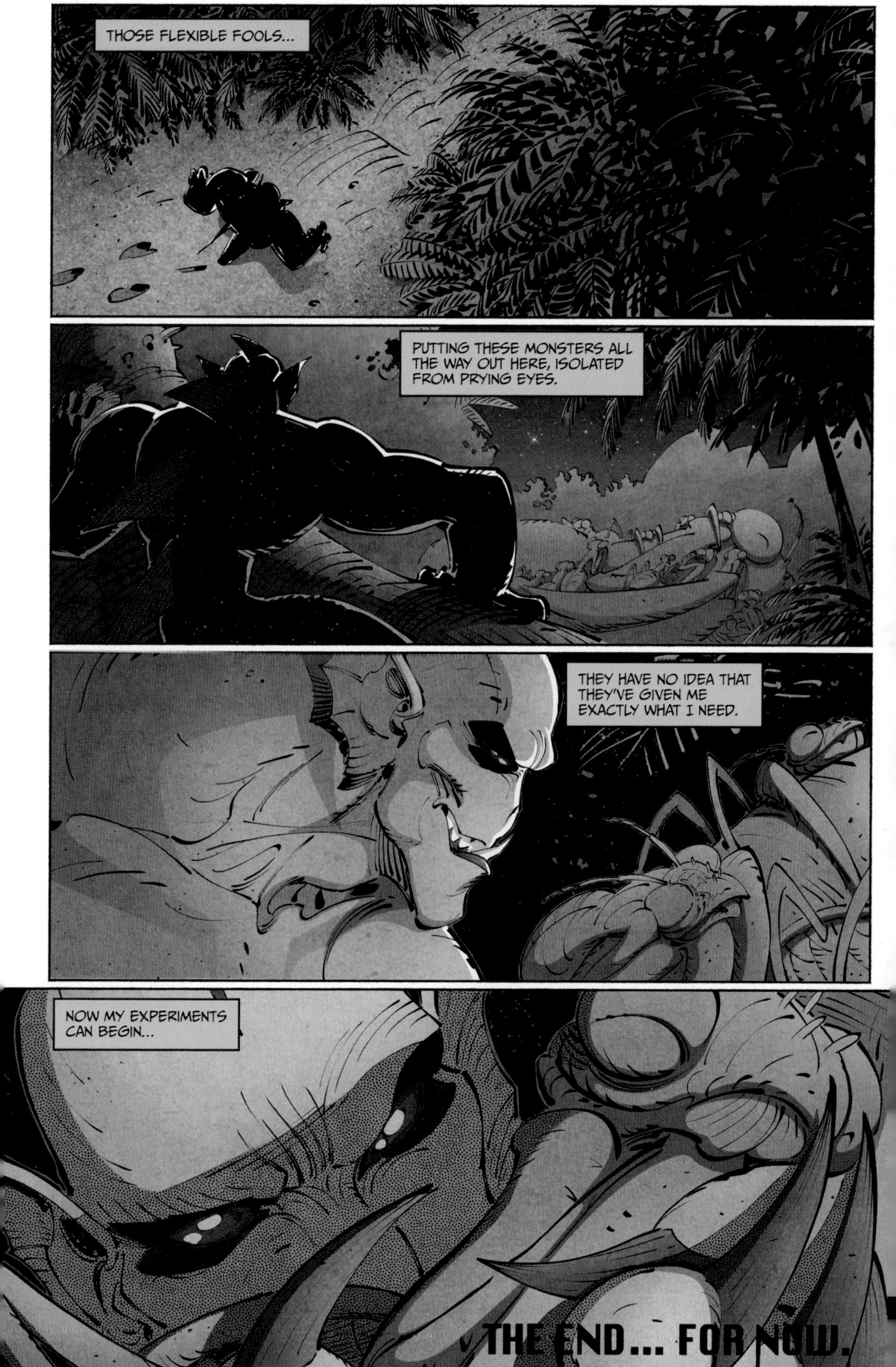
THOSE FLEXIBLE FOOLS...
PUTTING THESE MONSTERS ALL THE WAY OUT HERE, ISOLATED FROM PRYING EYES.
THEY HAVE NO IDEA THAT THEY'VE GIVEN ME EXACTLY WHAT I NEED.
NOW MY EXPERIMENTS CAN BEGIN...
THE END... FOR NOW.

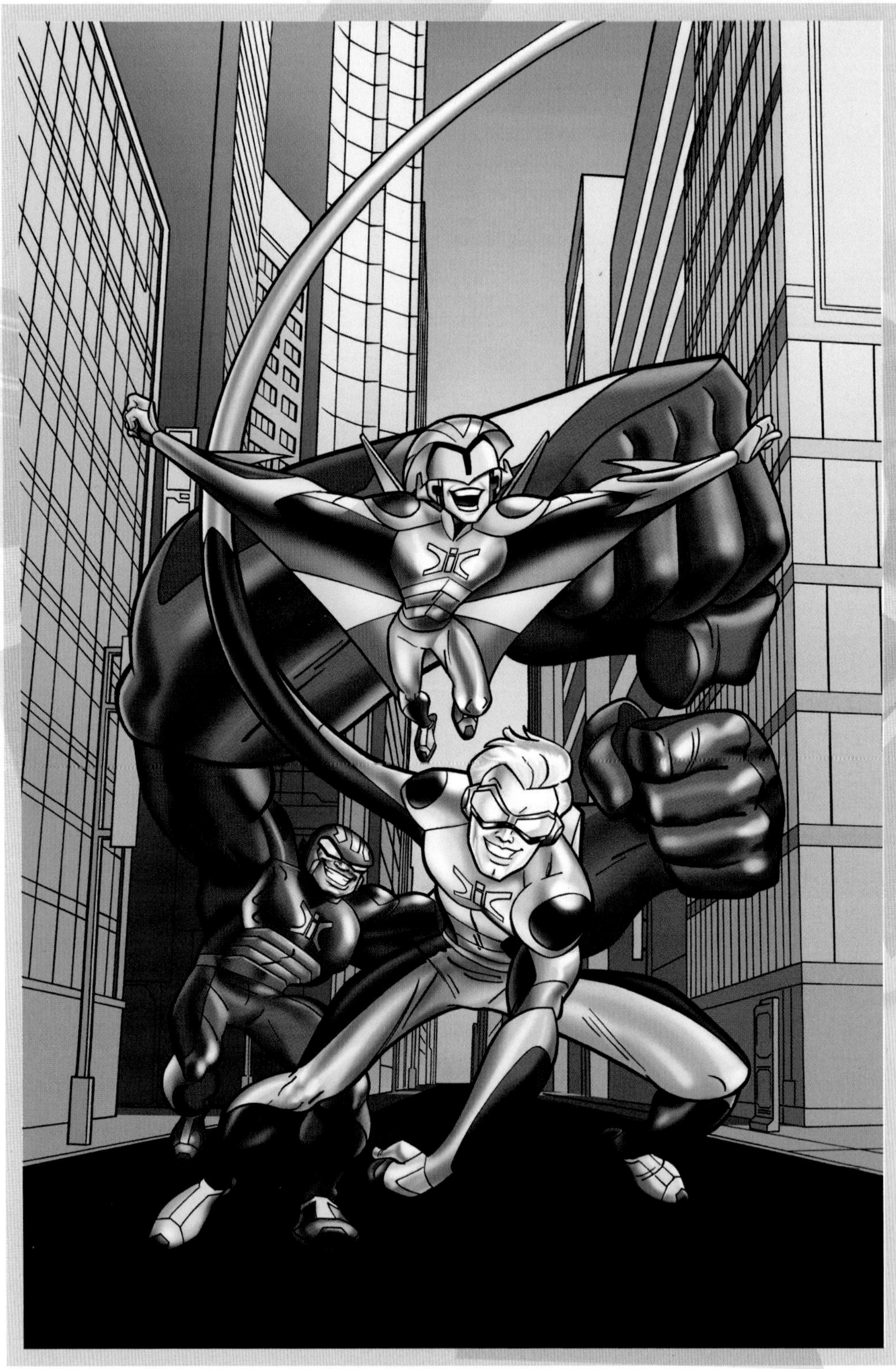

COVER ART
ALUIR AMANCIO

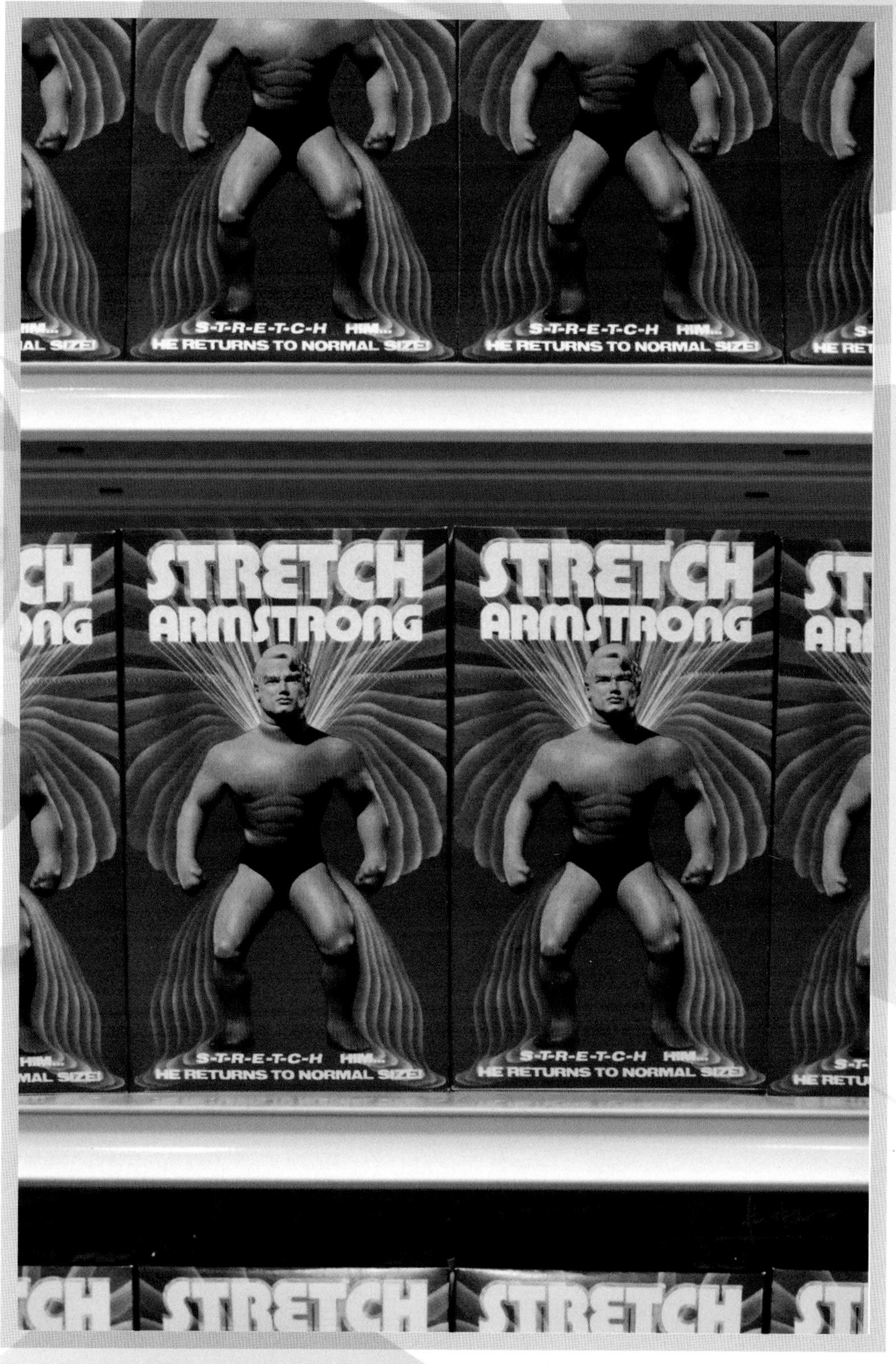
S-T-R-E-T-C-H HIM...
HE RETURNS TO NORMAL SIZE!
STRETCH
ARMSTRONG
S-T-R-E-T-C-H HIM...
HE RETURNS TO NORMAL SIZE!
STRETCH
ARMSTRONG
S-T-R-E-T-C-H HIM...
HE RETURNS TO NORMAL SIZE!
STRETCH
STRETCH

COVER ART
ADAM RICHES

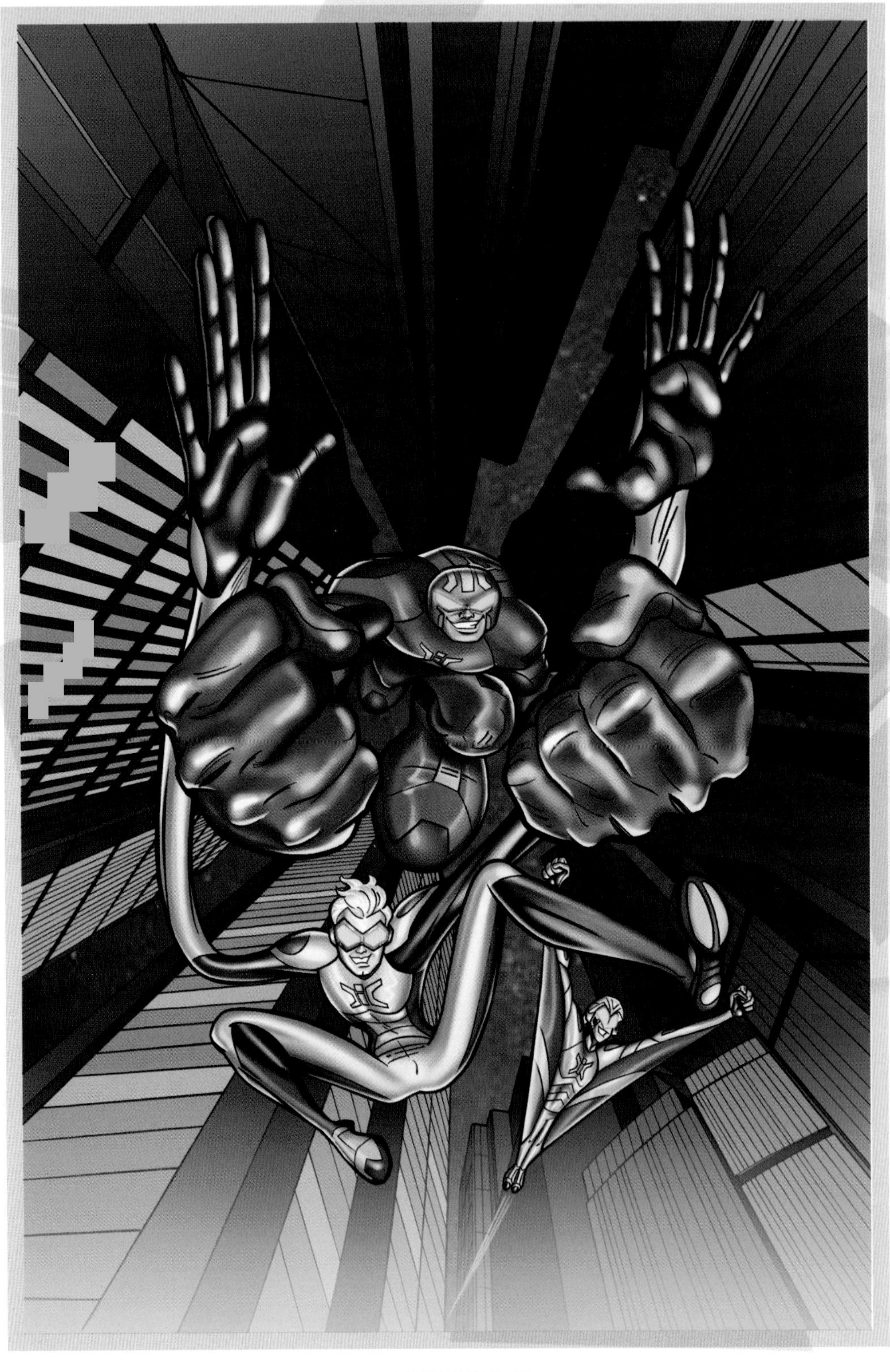

COVER ART
ALUIR AMANCIO

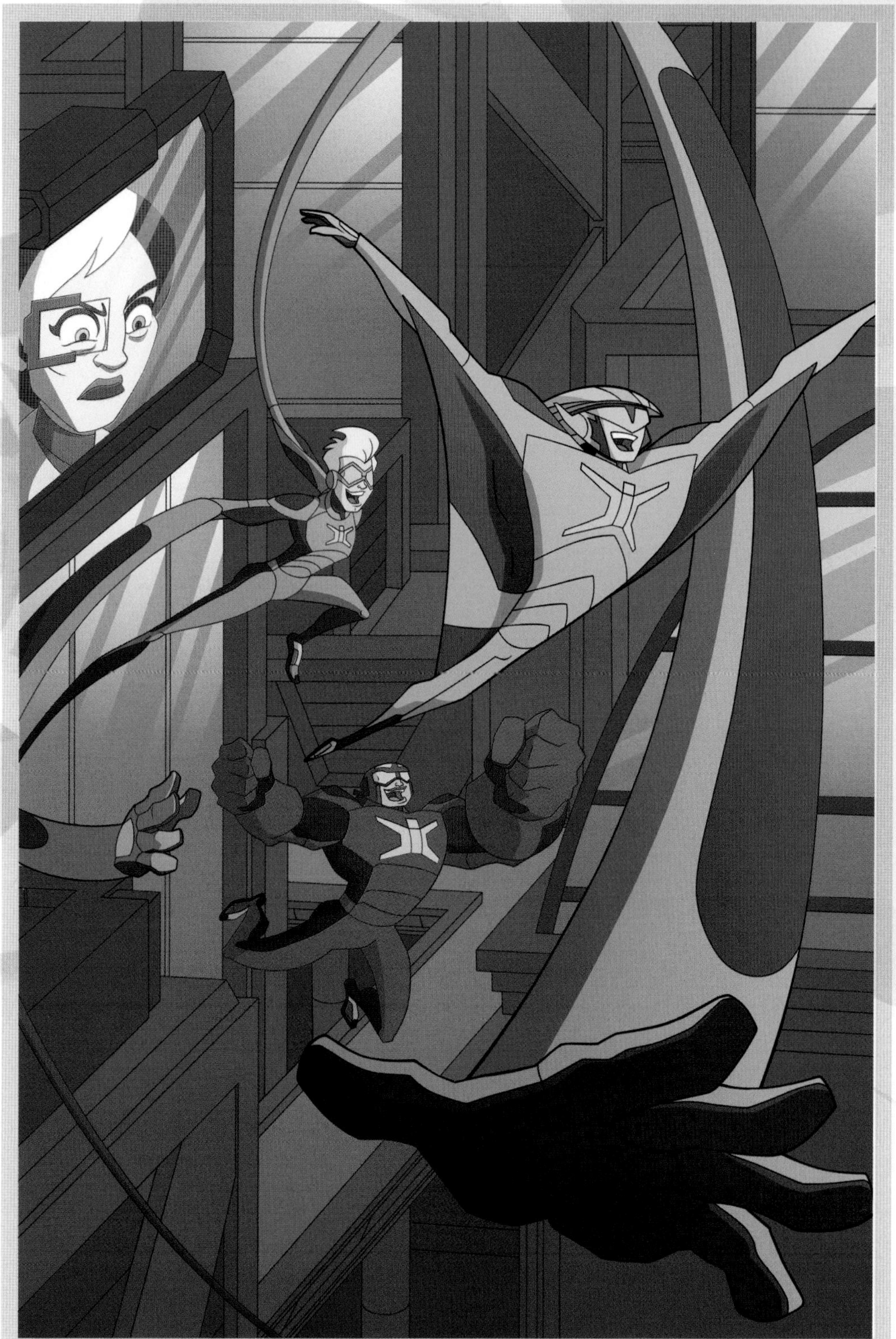

COVER ART
PHILIP MURPHY

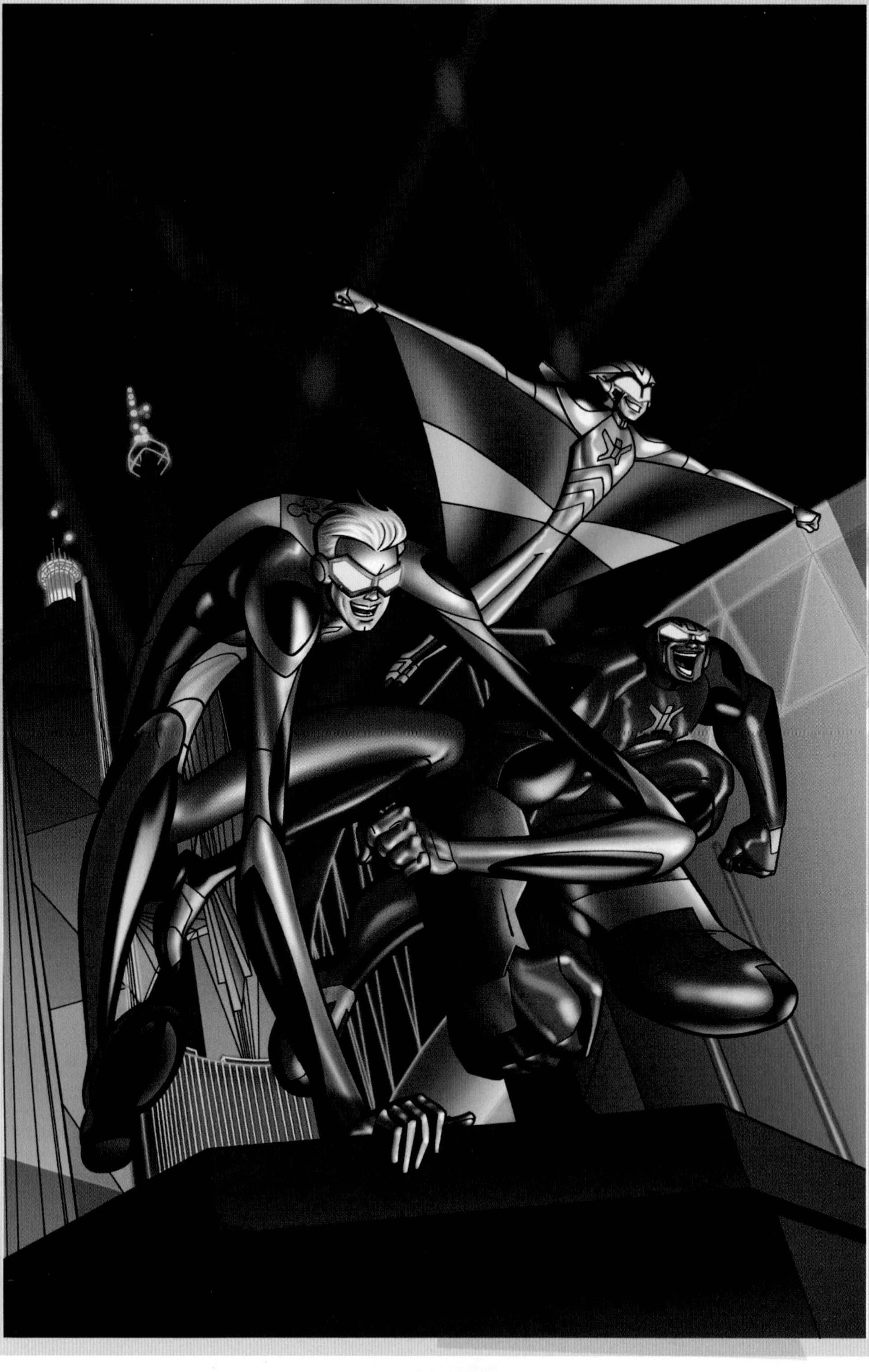

COVER ART
ALUIR AMANCIO